MADAME THÉRÈSE

OR

THE VOLUNTEERS OF '92

DOCTOR JACOB WAGNER.

MADAME THÉRÈSE

OR

THE VOLUNTEERS OF '92

TRANSLATED FROM THE FRENCH OF

ERCKMANN-CHATRIAN

ILLUSTRATED

NEW YORK
CHARLES SCRIBNER'S SONS
1900

TROW DIRECTORY
PRINTING AND BOOKBINDING COMPANY
NEW YORK

LIST OF ILLUSTRATIONS

INTRODUCTORY NOTE

THE public interest at the present time in the classics of French literature is sufficient, in the publishers' opinion, to warrant the issue of a new edition of the National Novels of MM. Erckmann-Chatrian. These novels, indeed, belong to the comparatively small number of literary productions of first-rate importance in their special sphere which can yet be transferred from one language to another with entire adequacy. They lend themselves especially to the English idiom because their color is that of the borderland between things French and things German, and therefore often not unlike that of much English literature comparable with them. MM. Erckmann-Chatrian long since became French classics. Every one knows their Alsatian origin, the peculiarly racy quality of both their style and the substance it clothes, their unique position in contemporary French literature, their long-con-

tinued, patient and finally triumphant struggle to
obtain it. But the cycle of stories known as " Romans Nationaux," is noteworthy in itself and of
particular interest to the American public for other
and more significant reasons than purely literary or
romantic ones.

The series of National Novels, indeed, is very
much more than a series of simple and affecting tales
with more form than German and more flavor than
French stories of a similar sort. It comprises six
chapters of familiar chronicle of the most valuable
kind, concerned for the most part with one of the
most interesting epochs of history—that of the
French Revolution and the First Empire. Each
book describes public events of the first importance
from the stand-point of an actor in them and, thus,
together they give one a picture of the wars of the
First Republic and of Napoleon of remarkable
vividness and reality. But this again would not
make the series as noteworthy as it is, if this were
its sole or its main characteristic. The novels, in
fact, are, further, so many historical pictures com-
posed not at hap-hazard nor for their pictorial value
alone, but in illustration of consistent and con-
firmed principles of political philosophy.

In these novels at all events MM. Erckmann-

Chatrian are publicists as well as romancers. "Madame Thérèse," for example, preaches eloquently the ardent proselyting republicanism of 1793. "The Conscript" shows the change in the popular feeling of Europe toward France, produced by the Napoleonic conquests, and in the popular feeling of France toward Napoleon by the constant state of warfare, the constant call for men and the consequent exhaustion of the country. "The Plébiscite" is a scorching exposure of the hollowness, corruption, and baseness of the policy responsible for the disasters of 1870-71. Each is not only a vivid picture, that is to say, but a picture with a pregnant moral. Taken as a whole the six novels form one of the most powerful and persuasive presentations that have ever been made of French republicanism, eulogizing its early exaltation and denouncing with equal vigor its betrayal by the Bonapartes and the open antagonism of it by the Bourbons.

Both picture and lesson are especially effective because both are drawn from the stand-point as well as in the interest of the people rather than from that of the literary artist or the impersonal historian. Not only is the fictitious narrator in each case an eye-witness of the events he chronicles; he is also a

member of the class which sees the most of war and
suffers most from it. In " Madame Thérèse " it is
the little Fritzel who describes the effect of the rev-
olutionary rise of the people and the warlike prop-
agandism of the gospel of liberty and fraternity.
In "The Conscript " it is the jeweller's lame appren-
tice who tells the story of the ill-advised and ill-
fated Russian expedition and of the subsequent disasters of the campaign of 1813.   In " The Blockade
of Phalsbourg " it is the shrewd Jew wine-seller who
narrates the hardships of the memorable siege.   In
" Waterloo," the Conscript of two years before is
again conscripted and relates the wide-spread dis-
content with the stupid rule of the restored Bourbons, the ill-treatment of the old soldiers, the national enthusiasm over the return from Elba, the
national depression on realizing that Napoleon's re-
accession meant perpetual war, the dramatic events
of the Hundred Days and their crowning catas-
trophe.   In " The Plébiscite " it is a miller, the
maire of his Alsatian village and a type of the millions of *petites gens* deceived by the epigram " the
Empire is peace," who describes the cynical policy
of Napoleon III.'s later days and the terrible re-
verses that were the inevitable consequence of bad
faith at home and ignorance of the situation abroad.

We learn from each volume how the *people* felt,
and what they thought, how they were affected—
benefited, used, betrayed, in succession—by the
great changes of the century since '89. Historical
archives, in consequence, contain no more important
historic testimony than this fiction, and the modern
democratic spirit has no finer, no more rational and
elevated expression than it obtains in these stories.

On the other hand, their historic worth does not
at all obscure the literary attractiveness of the National Novels. They are not only admirable contri-
butions to familiar history of a most convincing
and conclusive sense of reality; nor are they merely
besides this an eloquent exposition of the people's
gospel: they are, in the same rank with such other
works of their authors as " Friend Fritz " and " The
Polish Jew," for example, literary masterpieces of
a very high order. The depiction of character is
very sympathetic and very telling. Each personage
is evidently studied from the life, and illustrates a
type rather than an exception. The color of each
story is as delightfully harmonious as it is tenderly
subdued. The sentiment—supplied doubtless by
the German temperament of the authors in more
generous measure and more winning way than are
characteristic of most French literature of the kind

—is qualified and refined by their French training and literary traditions, with the result of a very agreeable compromise. There are evidences on every page of a simplicity which springs from this sane and contained but still penetrating sentiment, and which is an infallible mark of the truest literary distinction. In a word, the novels are marked equally by heart and by taste.

The narrative, moreover, is always admirably in character. The lucrative shrewdness of the sharp Hebrew speculator in " The Blockade of Phalsburg " is not dissembled; the unheroic love of peace appears as prominent in the Conscript as his domesticity and industry. And, through a similar rectitude of literary conscience, there is a very noteworthy impartiality shown in places where one might reasonably expect in a " national novel " the bias of patriotism. The Conscript noting, for example, that the Prussians at Waterloo " kill without mercy," immediately adds, " just as we did at Ligny "; and no opportunity is neglected of pointing out the reasonableness of the German, Austrian, and Cossack retaliation in 1813-14 for the French treatment of themselves during the years when they were the conquered. In fine, MM. Erckmann-Chatrian have more respect for their art than disposition

to appeal to the sensibility or the prejudice of their
readers; and the result, of course, is that in this
way the effect is greatly heightened, and that both
as literature and as history the absence of every
meretricious element and the presence of an absolute
candor cause the National Novels to take in their
field the very highest rank. The present edition can
but confer a public service in contributing to a
clearer public comprehension of a great movement
by a great people, described in the sympathetic but
impartial terms of literary artists of the first class.

" Madame Thérèse " begins the series, and is perhaps the most romantic. The scene is laid in a little
town of the Vosges which witnesses bloody conflicts
between the Republican soldiers and the Croats and
Cossacks of the Allies attacking France in 1793 in
behalf of the restoration of the Bourbons. It is an
extraordinarily vivid picture of the events and also
of the popular feeling of the time. Nowhere is
there a more striking presentation of the way in
which what were then called " the new ideas " were
disseminated not only throughout France, but
among the feudally oppressed of contiguous countries. Nor is there anywhere else a more sympathetic account of how popular and universal was the

enthusiasm which filled the French armies with
volunteers and enabled Carnot to " organize victory." Madame Thérèse herself is a *cantinière* of
the Republican cohorts, and her adventures are as
entertaining from the personal and human point of
view as the events among which they took place are
historically interesting.

MADAME THÉRÈSE

I

WE lived in profound quiet in the village of Anstatt, in the midst of the German Vosges,—my
uncle, Dr. Jacob Wagner, his old servant Lisbeth,
and I. After the death of his sister Christine,
Uncle Jacob had taken me to live with him. I was
nearly ten years old; fair, fresh and rosy as a
cherub. I used to wear a cotton cap, a little brown
velvet jacket made of a pair of my uncle's old
breeches, gray linen pantaloons, and wooden shoes
adorned on the top by a tuft of wool.

They called me little Fritzel in the village, and
every evening when Uncle Jacob returned from his
visits he used to take me on his knee, and teach me
to read, in French, from Buffon's Natural History.

It seems to me as if I were still in our low room,
with its ceiling crossed by beams blackened with
smoke. I see on my left, the little entry door and
the oaken chest of drawers; on the right, the alcove

closed by a curtain of green serge; in the back part
of the room, the entrance to the kitchen, near the
cast-iron stove, with heavy mouldings representing
the twelve months of the year; and toward the
street the two little windows, hung with vine leaves,
that opened on the square of La Fontaine.

I see my Uncle Jacob also, a slender man, his
high forehead crowned with beautiful fair hair,
which clustered gracefully around his prominent
temples,—his nose slightly aquiline, his eyes blue,
with a chin rounded, and lips tender and kind. He
wears black frieze breeches, and a sky-blue coat with
copper buttons. Seated in his leathern arm-chair,
he is reading with his elbows on the table, and the
sunlight makes the shadows of the vine leaves play
upon his face, which is somewhat long, and tanned
by exposure.

He was a kind-hearted man, and a lover of peace;
nearly forty years old, and considered the best physician in the neighborhood. I have learned since,
that he busied himself a great deal in theorizing
about universal brotherhood, and that the bundle
of books which Fritz the carrier brought him from
time to time treated of this important matter.

All this I see, not forgetting Lisbeth, a good old
dame, smiling and wrinkled, in a blue linen short

gown and petticoat, who sits in a corner and spins; nor do I forget the cat Roller, who dreams, seated on her tail, behind the stove, her great yellow eyes opened in the gloom like an owl's.

It seems to me that I have only to cross the lane to slip into the orchard, with its delicious fragrance; only to climb the wooden staircase to reach my room where I let loose the tomtits that Hans Aden the shoemaker's son, and I, had caught in snares. Some were blue and some were green. Little Eliza Meyer, the burgomaster's daughter, often came to see them and to ask me about them. When Hans Aden, Ludwig, Frantz Sépel, Karl Stenger and I led the cows and goats to pasture, on the Birkenwald hill, Eliza always pulled my jacket and said:

"Fritzel, let me lead your cow—don't send me off."

And I would give her my whip, and we would make a fire on the turf and roast potatoes in the ashes. Oh, the good old times! How calm, how peaceful was everything around us! How regularly all went on! Nothing disturbed our quiet Monday, Tuesday, Wednesday; every day of the week passed exactly like every other day.

Every day we rose at the same hour, dressed, and sat down to the good porridge prepared by Lisbeth.

Then my uncle went away on horseback, and I went out to set traps and snares for the thrushes, sparrows, or greenfinches,—according to the season. At noon we met again, and for dinner had bacon and cabbage and *noudels* or *knœpfels*. After dinner I went to the pasture to look after my traps, or to bathe in the Queich when it was warm. In the evening we had good appetites, and at the table thanked God for his goodness. Every day, when supper was nearly over, and it began to grow dark in the room, a heavy step crossed the passage, the door opened, and on the threshold appeared a short, thick, squarely-built, broad-shouldered man, wearing a large felt hat.

"Good-evening, doctor."

"Be seated, mole-catcher," my uncle would reply. "Lisbeth, open the kitchen door."

Lisbeth pushed open the door, and the red flame dancing on the hearth showed us the mole-catcher standing opposite the table, watching our supper with his little gray eyes. He looked just like a field-rat with his long nose, small mouth, retreating chin, straight ears, and thin, bristling, yellow moustache. His gray linen frock only reached partly down his back, and his great red waistcoat with deep pockets hung loosely over his hips. His immense shoes, covered with yellow earth, had large nails in them, which looked in front like shining claws all around his thick soles.

He looked fifty years old; his hair was turning gray, his ruddy forehead was deeply wrinkled, and his eyebrows, white with streaks of yellow, hung over his eyes.

He was always in the fields, setting his traps, or at the door of his apiary on the hill-side in the heath of the Birkenwald, with his wire mask and great linen mittens, and the broad sharp-edged spoon with which he took the honey from the hives. At the close of autumn he would leave the village for a month, his wallet on his back, a large pot of honey on one side, and on the other cakes of yellow wax which he sold to the clergy in the neighborhood, for their wax tapers. Such was the mole-catcher.

After looking steadily at the table for a time, he would say, " There is cheese—and there are nuts."

" Yes," my uncle would answer, " at your service."

" Thanks! I would rather smoke my pipe now." Then he would draw from his pocket a black pipe with a copper lid and chain attached; fill it with care,—still looking at us,—go into the kitchen, take a burning coal in the hollow of his hard hand, and place it on the tobacco. I see him, now, with his rat-like face, his nose upturned, blowing great puffs before the gloomy fire-place, then coming back and seating himself in the shadow at the corner of the stove, with his legs crossed. Besides moles and bees, honey and wax, the mole-catcher had another serious occupation:—he predicted the future by means of the flight of birds, the abundance of grasshoppers and caterpillars, and certain traditions inscribed in a large book with wooden covers which he had inherited from an old aunt in Héming, and which informed him of future events. But he would not enter upon the subject unless Koffel were present,—Koffel the joiner, the turner, the watchmaker, the shearer of dogs, and healer of animals;—in short, the finest genius of Anstatt, and the neighborhood. Koffel was a Jack of all trades. He wired broken crockery, tinned saucepans, repaired damaged furniture, and even the organ, when the pipes or bellows were out of order; and Uncle Jacob had been obliged to forbid his setting broken arms and legs, for he had also a talent for surgery, he thought. The mole-catcher admired him very much, sometimes saying, " What a shame that Koffel has not studied! What a shame!" And all the gossips in the place thought him a universal genius. But all this did not " make the pot boil," and the surest of his resources after all was to cut cabbage for sour-krout in autumn, carrying his tool-chest, on his back wallet-fashion, and crying from door to door, " Any cabbage? Any cabbage? "

Such is the fate of genius. Koffel, diminutive, meagre, with his black beard and hair, and his sharp nose pointed like the beak of a teal, was not long in coming—his hands in the pockets of his little short jacket, a cotton cap far back on his head, with the point between his shoulders, and his breeches and coarse blue stockings spotted with glue, hanging loosely on his thin wiry legs, his old shoes cut in several places to make room for his bunions. He came in a few minutes after the mole-catcher, and approaching the table with short steps, said gravely:

" A good appetite to you, doctor."

" Will you not share our meal with us? " asked my uncle.

" Many thanks. We had salad, to-night; that is what I like best."

Saying this, Koffel would seat himself behind the stove, and never stir until my uncle said, " Light the candle, Lisbeth, and take away the cloth."

Then he filled his pipe in his turn, and drew near the stove. They talked of the weather, the crops, etc. The mole-catcher had set so many traps that day, had turned off the water from such a meadow during the storm, or else he had taken so much honey from the hives; the bees would soon swarm; they were getting ready, and he was preparing beforehand baskets to receive the young.

Koffel was always pondering over some invention; he told of his clock without weights, from which the twelve apostles would come out at the stroke of noon, while the cock crowed, and death mowed with his scythe; or of his plough, which would go alone, wound up like a clock, or some other wonderful discovery. My uncle would listen gravely, nodding his head in approval, but thinking meanwhile of his patients. In summer, the women of the neighborhood, seated on the stone bench under the open windows, chatted with Lisbeth about household matters. One had woven so many yards of linen in the winter; the hens of another had laid so many eggs that day, and so on.

For myself, I seized a favorable moment to run off to Klipfel's forge, whose fire shone far off, at night, at the end of the village. There I always met Hans Aden, Frantz Sépel and several others. We watched the sparks flying from the heated iron under the strokes of the hammer; we whistled to the sound of the anvil. If a quiet old horse came to be shod, we helped to hold up his leg. Some of the older boys made themselves sick trying to smoke walnut leaves. Others boasted of going every Sunday to the dance. These were fifteen or sixteen years old. They wore their hats on one side, and smoked with an important air, with their hands deep down in their pockets. At ten o'clock we separated, and everybody went home. Most days passed thus, but Mondays and Fridays, the Frankfort Gazette came, and then the gatherings at our house were large. Besides the mole-catcher and Koffel came our burgomaster Christian Meyer, and M. Karolus Richter, the grandson of an old valet of Count Salm-Salm's. None of these people would subscribe for the Gazette, but they liked to hear it read for nothing.

How often since then I have called to mind the burly burgomaster, with his red ears, wearing a woollen jacket and cotton nightcap, sitting in the arm-chair—my uncle's accustomed seat. He seemed to be thinking profoundly, but was really intent upon remembering the news to impart to his wife, the excellent Barbara, who ruled the parish in his name. And the great Karolus, a sort of greyhound in hunting-coat and cap of boiled leather, the greatest usurer in the country, who looked down upon all the peasants from the height of his grandeur because his grandfather had been a lackey of Salm-Salm; who thought he did you a great favor in smoking your tobacco, and talked incessantly of parks and preserves, great hunts and the rights and privileges of my Lord Salm-Salm. How many times have I seen him in my dreams, marching up and down our room, listening, frowning, suddenly plunging his hand into the great pocket of my uncle's coat, for his tobacco, filling his pipe, and lighting it at the candle, saying, " By your leave." All these things I see again.

Poor Uncle Jacob! how good-natured he was to let his tobacco be smoked! But he paid no attention, apparently, so absorbed was he in the day's news. The Republicans were invading the Palatinate; were descending the Rhine. They dared to defy the three Electors, King William of Prussia, and the Emperor Joseph. Their audacity astonished our circle. M. Richter said this state of things could not last; these wicked beggars would be exterminated to the last man. When my uncle fin-

ished, he would make some judicious reflection. As
he refolded the paper he would say:

"Let us thank God that we live in the midst of
the forest rather than in the vineyards—on the
bleak mountain rather than in the fertile plain.
These Republicans can hope for no plunder here,
this is our security. We can sleep in peace. But
how many are exposed to their ravages! They do
everything by force; but no good ever comes of
force. They talk to us of love, equality and liberty, but they do not apply these principles. They
trust to their arms, and not to the justice of their
cause. Long ago, before their time, others came
to deliver the world. They struck no blows, they
took no lives, they died by thousands, and their
symbol in all succeeding ages has been the lamb,
devoured by wolves. One would think that not
even a single memorial of these men would remain.
Well, they conquered the world; they conquered
not the body, but the soul of man. And the soul
is all. Why do not these men follow their example?"

Karolus Richter immediately rejoined, with a
contemptuous air:

"Why? because they laugh at souls and envy
the powerful of the earth. And besides, these Re-

publicans are atheists, every man of them. They
respect neither throne nor altar. They have over-
turned the established order of things from the
beginning of time. They will have no more nobility; as if the nobility were not the very essence
of things on earth and in heaven; as if it were
not acknowledged by mankind that some were born
to be slaves and others to be rulers; as if we did
not see this order established even in nature. The
mosses are beneath the grass, the grass beneath the
bushes, the bushes beneath the trees, and the trees
beneath the starry sky. Just so are the peasants
under the merchants, the merchants under the
gownsmen, the gownsmen under the military nobles,
the military nobles under the king, the king under
the pope, represented by his cardinals, archbishops,
and bishops. This is the natural order of things.
A thistle can never grow to the height of an oak; a
peasant can never wield the sword like the descen-
dant of an illustrious race of warriors. These Republicans have obtained transient success, because
they have surprised everybody by their incredible
audacity and their want of common sense. In
denying all doctrines and all acknowledged rules,
they have stupefied reasonable men—hence these
disorders. Just as sometimes an ox or a bull stops

suddenly, then flies at the sight of a rat which unexpectedly comes up from the ground before him,
so are our soldiers astounded and even put to flight
by such audacity. But this cannot last, and after
the first surprise is over, I am very sure that our old
generals of the Seven Years War will defeat ut-
terly this disorderly crowd of wretches, and that not
one of them will return to his unfortunate country."

Having said this, M. Karolus relighted his pipe,
and continued his walk up and down with long
strides, his hands behind him, and a self-satisfied
air.

All reflected upon what they had just heard, and
the mole-catcher finally spoke in his turn.

"All that ought to happen, happens," said he.
"Since these Republicans have driven away their
lords and their priests, it was so ordained in heaven
from the beginning of time; 'God willed it.' Now,
whether they return or not depends upon what the
Lord God wills. If He chooses to raise the dead,
that depends on Him alone. But last year, as I
watched my bees working, I saw, all of a sudden,
these little gentle and pretty creatures fall upon
the drones, sting them and drag them out of the hive.
These drones produce the young, and the bees keep
them so long as the hive needs them, but then they

kill them. It is abominable; but nevertheless it is written! Seeing this, I thought of these Republicans. They are disposed to kill their drones ; but be tranquil; we can't live without them; others will come. They must be feathered and fed anew; after that the bees will get angry again, and kill them by hundreds. We think they are exterminated, but more will come, and so it goes on. It must be so! It must be so! "

Then the mole-catcher shook his head, and M. Karolus, stopping in the midst of his walk, cried:

" Whom do you call drones? The true drones are the conceited reptiles, who believe themselves capable of anything, and not the nobles and priests."

" Begging your pardon, M. Richter," replied the mole-catcher, " the drones are those who wish to do nothing and to enjoy everything; those who, without rendering any service except buzzing around the queen, wish to be generously provided for. They are cared for, but at last, it is written, they must be cast out. It has happened thousands of times and it must happen always. The working bees, orderly and economical, cannot support creatures that are good for nothing. It is unfortunate—it is sad. But so it is. When we make honey we like to keep it for ourselves.

" You are a Jacobin! " cried Karolus, angrily.

" No, on the contrary, I am a merchant of An-statt, a mole-catcher and raiser of bees. I love my country as well as you. I would sacrifice myself for her, perhaps, sooner than you would. But I am forced to say that the true drones are those who do nothing, and the true bees those who work, for I have seen it a hundred times."

" Ah," cried Karolus Richter, " I wager that Koffel has the same ideas as you! "

Then the little joiner, who had said nothing, re-plied, winking one eye:

" M. Karolus, if I had the happiness of being the grandson of a servant of Yéri-Peter or Salm-Salm, and if I had inherited great wealth which would support me in abundance and idleness, then I should say that the drones are the workers, and the bees the lazy ones. But, situated as I am, I have need of everybody's help, and so I say nothing. I am silent. Only I think that every one ought to have what he earns by his labor."

" My dear friends," said my uncle, gravely, " we will not speak of these things, for we cannot under-stand them. Peace! peace! that is what we must have. It is peace that makes men prosper, and puts them all in their true place. In war bad instincts prevail; murder, rapine, and the rest. Besides, all men who lead bad lives love war; it is the only way they can appear to be anything. In time of peace, they would be nothing; we would see too easily through their thoughts, their tricks and their desires. Man has been created by God for peace, for labor, the love of his family, and the like. But since war opposes all these it is truly a scourge. The clock has struck ten; we could discuss the subject until to-morrow morning without understanding it better. I propose, therefore, that we go to bed."

Then everybody rose, and the burgomaster, placing his two great hands on the arm of his chair, cried:

" God grant that neither the Republicans, nor Prussians, nor Imperialists pass through here, for they are all hungry and thirsty. And as it is more agreeable to drink our own wine than to see it swallowed by others, I would rather learn these things from the papers than see them with my own eyes. That is what I think."

With this remark, he moved toward the door; the others followed.

" Good-night," said my uncle.

" Good-night," replied the mole-catcher, disappearing in the dark street.

The door was closed, and my careful uncle said to me:

"Go to bed, Fritzel. Pleasant dreams."

"And you, too, uncle," I answered.

Lisbeth and I mounted the staircase. A quarter of an hour afterwards perfect silence reigned in the house.

II

One Friday evening, in the month of November, 1793, Lisbeth, after supper, was kneading the dough to make bread for the household, as usual. As it was to be used for cakes and apple-pies also, I kept near her in the kitchen, and as I watched her, gave myself up to the pleasantest dreams. When the dough was kneaded yeast was added, the kneading-trough carefully scraped, and a thick covering was spread over it, to let it ferment. Then Lisbeth scattered blazing coals from the hearth inside the oven, and pushed into it with the poker three great dry fagots, which soon began to blaze under the dark vaulted roof. Finally, when the fire was lighted, she closed the door of the oven and turned to me:

"Now, Fritzel, let us go to bed; to-morrow, when you wake up, there will be a pie for you."

We went up to our rooms. Uncle Jacob had been snoring for an hour in his alcove. I went to bed thinking of pies and cakes, and fell sound asleep immediately. I had slept for some hours, but it was still night, and the moon was shining brightly into my little window, when I was aroused by a strange tumult. It seemed as if the whole village were in commotion; doors were slamming in the distance; many footsteps were splashing through the muddy pools of the street; and I heard, too, people moving about in our house, and saw the purple reflection of lights on my window-panes. My alarm may be imagined. After listening awhile, I got quietly up, and opened a window. The street was full of people, and not only the street but the garden, and by-streets. I saw only large men with immense cocked hats, long blue coats with red facings, wide white belts, and large queues hanging down their backs, carrying sabres and cartridge-boxes, which I had never seen before. They had stacked their guns before our barn. Two sentinels guarded them. The others had already made themselves at home in the houses. In the stable three horses pawed the ground. Before Sépel's butcher shop, across the way, from the hooks in the wall on which calves were hung to be skinned, a whole ox was hanging,—his head and back dragging on the ground,—in the blaze of a great fire which lighted up the square. A man with his shirt-sleeves rolled up over his brawny arms was skinning him. He had cut him entirely open, and the blood was running and mixing with the mire of the street. The face of this man, with his bare throat and unkempt hair, was terrible to see.

I understood at once that the Republicans had unexpectedly entered the village, and while I was dressing I invoked the aid of the Emperor Joseph, of whom M. Karolus Richter so often spoke. The French had arrived during our first sleep, at least two hours before; for as I went down stairs I saw three of them, in their shirt-sleeves, like the butcher, taking the bread from our oven with the shovel. They had spared Lisbeth the trouble of baking, as their companions had spared Sépel the trouble of butchering. These men could do anything. Nothing embarrassed them. Lisbeth, seated in a corner, her hands crossed on her knees, watched them quite peacefully. Her first terror was over. Seeing me at the head of the stairs, she called out:

" Fritzel, come down. They will not hurt you."

Then I went down, and the men kept at their work without noticing me. The passage-door on the left was open, and I saw two more Republicans in the orchard mixing dough for a second or third batch of bread. Through the half-open door of the sitting-room, on the right, I saw Uncle Jacob sitting at the table, while a robust man, with large red whiskers, pug nose, projecting eyebrows, ears standing out from his head, and a tow-colored wig hanging down his back in a queue as thick as one's arm, was installed in the arm-chair, devouring one of our hams with evident relish. I could see his strong brown hands plying the knife and fork, and his muscular jaws moving. From time to time he raised his glass, took a good draught, and went on.

He wore lead-colored epaulettes, a large sabre, in a leathern sheath, whose guard rose behind his elbow, and boots which were hardly visible for the yellow mud which was beginning to dry upon them. From his hat on the sideboard, drooped red plumes which waved in the wind; for notwithstanding the cold, the windows were wide open. An armed sentinel paced up and down before them, stopping occasionally to glance at the table.

While carving the ham the man with large whiskers spoke roughly to my uncle.

" So you are a physician? "

" Yes, *monsieur le commandant.*"

" Call me simply colonel, or citizen colonel. I have already told you that ' *monsieur* ' and ' *madame* ' are out of fashion. But to return to our subject. You ought to know the country; a coun-

try physician is always on the road.   How far are
we from Kaiserslautern ? "

" Seven leagues, Colonel."

" And from Pirmasens ? "

" About eight."

" And from Landau ? "

" Five good leagues, I believe."

" ' I believe '—' nearly '—' about '—is it thus a
native of the country ought to speak ?   Listen : you
look as if you were afraid.   You are afraid that if
the white coats should come this way, they would
hang you for the information you give us.   You
may put that idea out of your head ; you are under
the protection of the French Republic."   And
looking Uncle Jacob in the face with his gray eyes :
" To the health of the Republic, one and indivisible ! " he cried, lifting his glass.

They touched glasses, and my uncle, very pale,
drank to the Republic.

" How is it," said the other, " you have not seen
any Austrians near here ? "

" No, Colonel."

" Are you very sure of it ?   Look me straight in
the face."

" I have not seen any."

" Did you not make a journey to Réethal,
lately ? "

My uncle had been to Réethal three days before. He thought that some one in the village had told the Colonel, and answered,

"Yes, Colonel."

"So; and were there no Austrians there?"

"No."

The Republican emptied his glass, casting a side-long glance at Uncle Jacob; then stretched out his arm, and took him by the wrist, with a strange expression.

"You say there were none?"

"Yes, Colonel."

"Well, you lie, then!" and in a slow voice he added: "*We* do not hang, but sometimes we shoot those who deceive us!"

My uncle's face became still paler, but he held up his head, and repeated in a firm tone:

"Colonel, I swear to you on my honor that there were no Imperialists at Réethal three days ago."

"And I," cried the Republican, his small gray eyes flashing under their thick, tawny brows, "I tell you that they were there! Is that plain?"

There was a silence. All in the kitchen had turned round; the Colonel's manner was not reassuring. I began to cry, and even went into the room, as if I could help Uncle Jacob, and placed myself behind him. The Republican looked at us, frowningly, which did not prevent him from swallowing another mouthful of ham, as if to give himself time for thought. Outside, Lisbeth sobbed aloud.

"Colonel," said my uncle, firmly, "perhaps you do not know that there are two Réethals, one on the road to Kaiserslautern, and the other on the Queich, three short leagues from Landau; the Austrians may have been at the lower one, but at the other, they had not been seen Wednesday evening."

"So!" said the Commandant, in bad Lorraine German, with a jeering smile, "that may be. But we from the country between Bitche and Sarreguemines, are as knowing as you. Unless you can prove to me that there are two Réethals, I will tell you that it is my duty to have you arrested, and tried by a court-martial."

"Colonel," cried my uncle, stretching out his arm, "the proof that there are two Réethals is that they are to be found on all the maps of the country."

He pointed to our old map, hanging on the wall. The Republican turned round, and looking at it, said:

"Ah, it is a map of the country! Let us examine it a little."

My uncle took the map down, and spreading it on the table, showed him the two villages.

" It is true," said the Colonel. " Well and good; I ask nothing better than to see a thing plainly."

He leaned his elbows on the table, and with his large head between his hands, looked at the map.

" Hold, hold! this is famous! " he said; " where did this map come from? "

" My father made it. He was a mathematician."

The Republican smiled.

" Yes; the woods, the rivers, the roads, all are marked," said he. " I recognize that we passed that place—it is good—very good! " Then straightening himself up: " You have no use for this map, citizen doctor," said he in German. " I need it, and I put it in requisition for the service of the Republic. Well, well, I beg your pardon. Let us have one drink more in honor of the Republic."

We can imagine with what eagerness Lisbeth went down into the cellar to find another bottle. Uncle Jacob had recovered his confidence. The Colonel, looking at me, asked:

" Is that your son? "

" No, he is my nephew."

" A well-built little fellow. It pleased me to see him come in just now to your aid. Come here, close," he said, drawing me to him by the arm. He passed his hand through my hair, and said, in a voice a little harsh, but kindly: " Bring up this boy in the love of the rights of man. Instead of taking care of cows, he may become colonel, or general, as well as anybody else. Now all the doors are open; any position can be taken. One need only have heart and luck to succeed. I, such as you see me, am the son of a blacksmith of Sarreguemines; but for the Republic, I should still hammer the anvil; our great lanky fellow of a count, who is with the white coats, would be an eagle by the grace of God, and I should be an ass. Instead of this, it is all the other way, thanks to the Revolution."

He emptied his glass brusquely, and half shutting his eyes with a crafty expression, added:

" That makes a little difference."

On the table, beside the ham, was one of our short-cakes which the Republicans had baked with the first batch of bread. He cut a piece for me, and said, very good-humoredly,

" Eat this boldly and try to become a man." Then turning toward the kitchen, " Sergeant Laflèche! " roared he, in a voice of thunder.

An old sergeant with gray moustaches, dry as a salt herring, appeared in the doorway.

" How many loaves, Sergeant ? "

" Forty."

" In an hour we must have fifty; with our ten ovens, five hundred,—three pounds of bread for each man."

The Sergeant went back to the kitchen. My uncle and I observed all this without moving. The Colonel again bent over the map, his head between his hands. Day began to dawn. The armed sentinel was still pacing up and down before our windows. Silence prevailed. Many of the soldiers were sleeping, their heads on their knapsacks, around the large fires which they had kindled; others were in the houses. The clock ticked slowly; the fire still sparkled in the kitchen. But in a few moments, a great noise arose in the street; window-panes crashed; a door was thrown open noisily, and we heard our neighbor, Joseph Spick, cry, " To the rescue! Fire! " But no one stirred in the village. All were glad to remain quietly in their own houses. The Colonel listened.

" Sergeant Laflèche! " cried he. The Sergeant had gone to see what the matter was. He came back in a moment. " What has happened? " asked the Colonel.

" It is an aristocrat of an inn-keeper, who re-

fuses to comply with the requisitions of the citizen
Thérèse," replied he, gravely.

" Very well! bring him to me."

The Sergeant went out. In a few minutes our
lane was full of people. The door reopened, and
Joseph Spick, in a short jacket, loose linen pantaloons, and a cap of curled wool, appeared between
four armed soldiers of the Republic, with faces yellow as gingerbread, worn-out hats, ragged elbows,
patched knees, and torn shoes, mended with twine;
all of which did not, however, prevent their holding up their heads high, as proud as kings. Joseph
Spick, his hands in his pockets, shoulders bent,
mouth open, and quaking cheeks, trembled so that
he could hardly stand on his long legs. He seemed
bewildered. Behind him, in the shadow, the head
of a woman, pale and thin, at once attracted my attention. She had a high forehead, straight nose,
long chin, and blue-black hair, which drooped in
large bands over her temples, and was braided behind the ears, so that her face seemed extremely
long. Her eyes were large, and black. She
wore a felt hat with the tri-color cockade, and
over it a red handkerchief knotted under the
chin. As I had seen, in our country, only blondes
or brunettes, this woman filled me with astonish-

ment and admiration. Young as I was, I looked at her amazed. My uncle appeared no less astonished than I, and after she had come in, followed by five or six other Republicans, dressed like the first, we could not take our eyes off of her.

She wore a large cloak of blue cloth, with a triple cape falling to the elbows, a little cask, which was hung over her shoulder, and around her neck a thick black silk cravat, with long fringe—doubtless some spoil of war—which heightened still more the beauty of her calm, proud face.

The Colonel waited until all had come in, looking closely at Joseph Spick, who seemed more dead than alive. Then turning to the woman, who had just raised her hat, with a movement of the head, said:

" Well, Thérèse, what has happened? "

" You know, Colonel, that at the last halting-place I had not another drop of brandy," said she, in a firm, clear voice. " My first care on arriving here, was to go through the village to find some, intending to pay for it, of course. But the people hid it all, and it was not until half an hour ago that I saw the fir-branch on this man's door. Corporal Merlot, Private Cincinnatus, and Drum-major Horatius Coclès followed, to help me. We went in and asked for wine, brandy, or anything of the kind; but the aristocrat had nothing; he was deaf. Then we searched the place, and at last found the entrance to the cellar, in the wood-house, concealed by a pile of fagots. We might have quarreled with him; instead of that, we went down, and found wine, bacon, sour-krout, and brandy. We filled our casks, took some bacon, and came up quietly. But seeing us return thus laden, this man, who was seated tranquilly in his room, began to cry for help, and instead of accepting my money, tore it up, and seizing me by the arm, shook me with all his strength. Cincinnatus put his load on the table, and taking this great fool by the collar, threw him against the window of his old house. Then Sergeant Laflèche arrived. That is all, Colonel."

When she had finished, she withdrew behind the others, and immediately a little dry man, thin and brusque, whose hat was on one side, and who held under his arm a long cane with a copper knob, shaped like an onion, came forward, and said, pompously:

" Colonel, what Citizen Thérèse has just communicated is an expression of the indignation which one naturally feels at coming in contact with a senseless aristocrat who thinks "——

MADAME THÉRÈSE.

"Very well," interrupted the Commandant, "the word of Citizen Thérèse is sufficient." And addressing Joseph Spick in German, he said, frowningly: "Tell me, do you wish to be shot? It will cost only the trouble of leading you into your garden. Do you not know that the paper of the Republic is worth more than the gold of tyrants? Listen; this time I will pardon you, in consideration of your ignorance; but if it happens that you again conceal your provisions, and refuse to accept our money in payment, I will have you shot in the village square to serve as an example to others. Go, then! march, you great idiot!"

He delivered this little harangue very emphatically. Then turning to the *cantinière*, said,

"Well, Thérèse, you can fill your cask; this man will make no further objections. And you, soldiers, release him."

They all went out. Thérèse first, Joseph last. The poor devil had hardly a drop of blood left in his veins. He had just had a narrow escape.

Meanwhile, daylight had come. The Colonel rose, folded the map, and put it into his pocket. Then he went to a window and looked out on the village. My uncle and I looked from the other window. It was about five o'clock in the morning.

III

As long as I live I shall remember that silent street, filled with sleeping men; some stretched out, some coiled up, their heads resting on their knapsacks. I can still see those muddy feet, those worn-out shoes, and patched coats, those young faces, tinged with brown, and rigid old faces, with closed eyelids; the large hats, faded epaulettes, the cockades, the woollen blankets with ragged red borders, the gray cloaks, and the straw scattered in the mud. Then the great silence of their sleep after the forced march—this absolute repose like death. All was enveloped in the bluish light of early morning; the pale sun, rising in a fog, shed but a sickly light over the little houses with their large thatched roofs, and small black windows. In the distance, at both ends of the village, on the Altenberg, and the Rée-pockel, above the orchards and hemp-fields, the sentinels' bayonets gleamed among the fading stars. No, I shall never forget that strange spectacle. I was very young then, but such memories are eternal.

As the day advanced, the picture became animated. One man raised his head, leaned on his elbow, and looked round; then yawned, and went to sleep again. Then an old soldier suddenly straightened himself, shook the straw from his clothes, adjusted his felt hat, and folded his ragged blanket; another rolled up his cloak and buckled it on his knapsack; a third drew from his pocket the stump of a pipe, and struck a light. The early risers had gathered together, and were talking, and the others joined them, stamping their feet, for it was cold at that hour, and the fires which had been lighted in the streets and on the Common had gone out.

Opposite our house, on the little square, was the fountain. Some of the Republicans were collected around two large moss-covered troughs, washing themselves, laughing, and chatting pleasantly, notwithstanding the cold; others were stooping down, drinking with upturned mouths from the pump.

Then the houses were opened, one by one, and we saw soldiers coming out from them, stooping so as not to strike their heads against the low doorways. Nearly all had their pipes lighted.

To the right of our barn, before Spick's inn, was stationed the *cantinière's* cart, covered with a large

3

cloth. It had two wheels, like a hand-barrow, the shafts lying on the ground.

The mule was behind, covered with an old woollen horse-blanket of red and blue check, and had drawn from our stall a long wisp of hay, which he chewed gravely with half-closed eyes and a sentimental air.

The *cantinièrc* was seated at the window mending a little pair of pantaloons, and throwing a glance from time to time at the shed, where the drum-major, Horatius Coclès, Cincinnatus, Merlot, and a tall, thin, dry, jovial fellow, were seated astride bundles of hay, making each other's queues. They combed out the braids, and smoothed them by spitting on their hands.

Horatius Coclès, who was the head of the band, was humming an air, and his comrades repeated the refrain.

Near them against two old casks slept a little drummer, about twelve years old, as fair as myself, who interested me particularly. It was he whom the *cantinière* was watching, and doubtless they were his pantaloons that she was mending. He was stretched out, his face upturned, his mouth half-opened, his back against the two casks and one arm over his drum. His drumsticks were slipped into his shoulder-belt, and on his feet, covered with straw, was stretched out a large, and very dirty spaniel, which kept him warm. Every moment this dog raised his head and looked at the boy, as if to say:

"I should like very much to take a tour among the kitchens of the village!"

But the little one did not stir, he slept so soundly! When some dogs barked in the distance the spaniel gaped. He would have liked to be one of the party.

Soon two officers came out of a neighboring house; two slender young men in tightly-fitting coats. As they passed the house, the Colonel cried:

"Duchêne! Richer!"

"Good-morning, Colonel," said they, turning back.

"Are the posts relieved?"

"Yes, Colonel."

"Nothing new?"

"Nothing, Colonel."

"In half an hour we begin our march. Sound the call, Richer. Come in, Duchêne."

One of the officers went in. The other passed into the shed and said something to Horatius Coclès. I looked at the new-comer. The Colonel had ordered a bottle of brandy. They were drinking together, when a hum was heard outside. It was the drum-beat. I ran to see what was going on. Horatius Coclès, at the head of five drummers—among whom, on the left, was the little boy—raising his baton, initiated the performance, which continued as long as he held it up. The Republicans came in from all the by-streets of the village, and were ranged in two lines in front of the fountain, and their sergeants began the call. My uncle and I were astonished at the order which prevailed among these men. When their names were called they answered so promptly that it seemed as if there were but one reply from all sides. They had taken their guns, and held them carelessly, on their shoulders, or with the butt-end on the ground,—just as they chose.

After the call there was perfect silence, and then several men from each company were detached, under the escort of the corporals, to go and fetch their bread. Citizen Thérèse harnessed her mule to the cart. Some moments afterwards the squads returned, bringing loaves of bread in bags and baskets. The distribution began. As the Republicans had made and eaten soup on their arrival, they were not hungry, and each one buckled a loaf to his knapsack.

" Come! " cried the Colonel, in a joyful tone, " let us move! "

He took his cloak, threw it over his shoulders, and
went out, without saying good-by to anybody.

We thought we had got rid of these people forever.

As soon as he had gone, the burgomaster came
to entreat Uncle Jacob to go home with him immediately, as the sight of the Republicans had made
his wife ill.

They went out together. Lisbeth at once arranged the chairs, and swept out the sitting-room.
We could hear the officers' commands outside.
"Forward, march!" The drums sounded. The
cantinière cried "*Huc!*" to her mule, and the
battalion was starting, when suddenly a terrible
cracking resounded through the village. It was
the firing of guns, sometimes several together,—
then one at a time.

The Republicans were just going into the street.
"Halt!" cried the Colonel, standing in his stirrups and looking around, listening attentively.

I went to the window, and saw all these men
attentive, and the officers outside the ranks, gathered around their chief, who was speaking with animation.

Suddenly a soldier appeared at the corner of the
street. He was running with his gun on his shoulder.

" Colonel," he called out, while still at a distance,
quite breathless, " the Croats! The outposts are
carried—they are coming! "

He had hardly finished speaking when the Colonel turned back, galloped along the line at full
speed, and cried:

" Form square! "

The officers, the drummers, and the *cantinière*,
all fell back, in front of the fountain, while the
companies crossed each other like the shuffling of a
pack of cards. In less than a minute they had
formed a square, three deep, with the others in the
middle. Immediately after, a terrible noise was
heard in the street; the Croats were coming; the
ground shook. I see them now pouring into the
street, their large red cloaks trimmed with fur floating behind them like banners, and bending so low
in their saddles with their sabres in front, that one
could hardly see the brown bony faces, with long
yellow moustaches.

It seems as if children must be possessed with the
devil, for instead of running to a place of safety,
I stayed there, with eyes wide-open to see the fight.
I was very much afraid, it is true, but curiosity
was stronger than fear.

While I looked and trembled, the Croats had

reached the square. Instantly the Colonel cried:
" Fire ! "

Then a clap of thunder, then nothing but a buzzing in my ears. Each side of the square turned
toward the street had fired at once; our window-
panes were shivered, the smoke came into the room,
with pieces of cartridges, and the smell of powder
filled the air. I, my hair standing on end, still
looked on, and saw the Croats on their small horses
rush forward in the gray smoke, fall back, then rush
forward again, as if trying to climb over the square,
and others coming up constantly, crying in a savage
voice:

" Forward! forward! "

" Fire, the second rank! " cried the Colonel, in
the midst of neighings and ceaseless cries. His voice
was as calm as when he was speaking in our room.
Another clap of thunder followed, and how the
plastering fell, how the tiles rattled from the roofs,
how heaven and earth seemed to mingle! Lisbeth,
in the kitchen, uttered screams so piercing that even
in all the tumult they could be heard like a shrill
whistle.

After the fire of the platoon, began the fire of
the file. We could see the guns of the second rank
lower, fire, then rise again, while the first rank,

with their knees bent on the ground, crossed bayonets, and the third loaded the guns and passed
them to the second. The Croats whirled round the
square striking from a distance with their long
sabres. From time to time a hat fell, sometimes
a man. One of the Croats, throwing his horse back
on his haunches, leaped so far that he cleared the
three lines, and fell inside the square. But then
the Republican Colonel threw himself upon him,
and with a furious stroke, nailed him, so to speak,
to the back of his horse. I saw him withdraw his
sabre red to the hilt. This sight made me turn cold.
I was going to fly, but had hardly risen, when the
Croats faced about, and fled, leaving a great number of men and horses in the square. The horses
tried to rise, then fell again. Five or six horsemen
lay under their beasts, trying to free their legs;
others, all bloody, dragged themselves along on all
fours, raising their hands, and crying in a lamentable voice, in their fear of being killed, " Pardon,
Frenchmen! " Some, not able to endure their sufferings, begged the favor of being put out of such
misery.

Most of them, however, lay motionless. For the
first time, I fully understood what death is; these
men that I had seen two minutes before, full of life

and strength, charging their enemies with fury, and rushing forward like wolves, lay there, pell-mell, senseless as the stones of the street.

In the ranks of the Republicans there were also vacant places, bodies stretched on their faces, and some wounded, their heads and faces covered with blood. They bandaged their heads, placing their guns at their feet, without leaving the ranks. Their comrades helped them to bind on a hand-kerchief, and put the hat above it. The Colonel, on horseback near the fountain, his large plumed hat pushed back, and his sabre clenched in his hand, closed up the ranks; near him were some drummers in line, and a little farther on, near the trough, was the *cantinière* with her cask. We could hear the trumpets of the Croats sounding the retreat. They had halted at the turn of the street. One of their sentinels was posted there, behind the corner of the Town Hall. Only his horse's head was to be seen. Some guns were still being fired.

"Cease firing!" cried the Colonel, and all was silent. We heard only the trumpet in the distance.

The *cantinière* then went inside the ranks to pour out brandy for the men, while seven or eight sturdy fellows drew water from a fountain in their bowls, for the wounded, who begged for drink in pitiable voices. I leaned from the window, looking down the deserted street, and asking myself if the red cloaks would dare to return. The Colonel also looked in that direction, and talked with a captain who was leaning against his saddle. Suddenly the captain crossed the square, left the ranks, and rushed into our house, crying:

" The master of the house? "

" He has gone out."

" Well—you—lead me to your garret—quick! "

I left my shoes there, and began to climb the steps at the end of the hall like a squirrel; the captain followed me. At the top, he saw at a single glance the ladder of the pigeon-house, and mounted before me. When we had entered, he placed his elbows on the edge of the somewhat low window, and leaned forward so as to see. I looked over his shoulder. The entire road, as far as one could see, was lined with men, cavalry, infantry, cannon, army wagons, red cloaks, green pelisses, white coats, helmets, cuirasses, files of lances and bayonets, ranks of horses, and all were coming toward the village.

" It is an army! " exclaimed the captain, in a low voice.

He turned suddenly to go down, then, seized with an idea, pointed out to me along the village, within two gunshots, a file of red cloaks who were turning the curve of the road just behind the orchards.

"You see those red cloaks?" said he.

"Yes."

"Does a carriage road pass there?"

"No, it is a foot-path."

"And this large hollow which cuts it in the middle, directly before us—is it deep?"

"Oh, yes!"

"Carriages and carts never pass that way?"

"No, they could not."

Then, without asking anything more, he descended the ladder backwards, as rapidly as possible, and hastened down the stairs. I followed him; we were soon at the foot, but before we had reached the end of the hall, the approach of a body of cavalry caused the houses to shake. Despite this, the captain went out, took two men from the ranks, and disappeared. Thousands of quick, strange cries, like those of a flock of crows, "Hurrah! hurrah!" filled the street from one end to the other, and nearly drowned the dull thud of the horses' galloping. I, feeling very proud of having conducted the captain to the pigeon-house, was so imprudent as to go to the door. The lancers, for this time they were lancers, came like the wind, their spears in rest, their ears covered by large hair caps, eyes staring, noses almost concealed by their moustaches, and large pistols, with butt ends of brass, in their belts. It was like a vision. I had only time to jump back from the door. My blood froze in my veins. And it was only when the firing recommenced that I awoke, as if from a dream, and found myself in the back part of our room opposite the broken windows. The air was thick, the square all white with smoke. The Colonel alone was visible, seated immovable on his horse near the fountain. He might have been taken for a bronze statue in this blue sea, from which hundreds of red flames spouted. The lancers leaped about like immense grasshoppers, thrust their spears, and withdrew them; others fired their pistols into the ranks, at four paces.

It seemed to me that the square was breaking. It was true.

" Close the ranks! stand firm! " cried the Colonel, in his calm voice.

" Close the ranks! Close! " repeated the officers all along the line. But the square gave way, and became a semi-circle. The centre nearly touched the fountain. At each stroke of the lance, the parry of the bayonet came like a flash of light, but some-

times the man fell. The Republicans no longer had
time to reload. They ceased firing, and the lances
were constantly coming, bolder, more numerous, en-
veloping the square in a whirlwind, and already uttering cries of triumph, for they believed themselves
conquerors.

For myself, I thought the Republicans were lost,
when, in the height of the combat, the Colonel, raising his hat on the end of his sabre, began to sing a
song which made one's flesh creep, and all the battalion, as one man, sang with him. In the twinkling
of an eye the whole front of the square straightened
itself, and forced into the street all the mass of
horsemen, pressed one against another, with their
long lances, like corn in the fields. This song seemed
to render the Republicans furious. It was terrible
to see them. And I have thought many times since
that men arrayed in battle are more ferocious than
wild beasts. But there was something still more
horrible; the last ranks of the Austrian column, at
the end of the street, not seeing what was passing
at the entrance of the square, rushed forward, crying, "Hurrah! hurrah!" so that those in the first
ranks, repulsed by the bayonets of the Republicans,
and not able to go further back, were thrown into
unspeakable confusion, and uttered distressing cries;

their large horses, pricked in the nostrils, were so frightened that their manes stood up straight, their eyes started from their heads, and they uttered shrill cries, and kicked wildly. From a distance I saw these unfortunate lancers, mad with fear, turn round, strike their comrades with the handles of their lances to force a passage for themselves, and fly like hares past the houses.

A few minutes afterward the street was empty. There remained, indeed, twenty-five or thirty poor devils shut up in the square. They had not seen the retreat, and were entirely disconcerted, not knowing where to fly. But this was soon over. A fresh discharge of the guns stretched them on their backs, except two or three who were thrown into Tanners' Lane. Only a heap of horses and dead men was to be seen. Blood flowed through the gutters, into the trough.

" Cease firing! " cried the Colonel, for the second time. " Load! "

At that moment nine o'clock struck from the church tower. It is impossible to describe the village as it looked then; houses pierced with balls; shutters hanging from their hinges; windows shattered; chimneys tottering; the street full of tiles and broken bricks, the roofs of the sheds open to the sky, and that heap of dead, those horses stretched on the ground, struggling and bleeding. It is a scene which defies description.

The Republicans, diminished by half their number, their large hats fallen back, stern and terrible in aspect, awaited orders under arms. Behind, at a little distance from our house, stood the Colonel, deliberating with his officers. I could easily hear what he said.

"We have an Austrian army before us," said he, abruptly. "The question is, how to save ourselves. In an hour we shall have twenty or thirty thousand men upon us. They will surround the village with their infantry, and we shall all be lost. I am going to beat a retreat. Has anybody anything to say?"

"No, it is a wise decision."

Then they disappeared, and two minutes after, I saw a number of soldiers enter the houses, throw chairs, tables, and chests of drawers into a heap outside; some threw straw and hay from the barns; others brought carts and carriages from the outhouses. In less than ten minutes they had formed at the entrance of the street a barrier as high as the houses; they placed hay and straw above and beneath it. The drum-beat recalled those who were engaged in this work. The fire rose immediately, step by step, to the top of the barricade, licking the neighboring roofs with its red flames, and spreading its black smoke like an immense vault over the village. Loud cries rose in the distance; shots were heard on the other side, but we saw nothing, and the Colonel gave the order for retreat. I saw the Republicans defile past our house with slow, firm steps, flashing eyes, red bayonets, black hands, hollow cheeks. Two drummers marched silently behind, one of whom was the little boy whom I had seen sleeping in our shed. He had his drum slung over his shoulder, and was bent forward, in marching attitude; large tears flowed over his round cheeks, which were blackened by the smoke of the powder. His comrade said, " Come, little Jean, courage! " But he did not seem to hear him. Horatius Coclès and the *cantinière* had disappeared. I followed the troop with my eyes until they turned the street. A few moments afterward the bell of the Town Hall sounded, and in the distance distressed voices were heard, crying, " Fire! fire! "

I looked toward the barricade of the Republicans. The fire had reached the houses, and rose toward the sky. On the other side the din of arms filled the street, and already long black pikes were thrust from the garret-windows of the neighboring houses to break down the burning barricade.

IV

AFTER the departure of the Republicans, a quarter of an hour passed before anybody appeared on our side of the street. All the houses seemed deserted. On the other side of the barricade the tumult increased; cries of " Fire! fire! " continued, in dismal tones. I went into the shed, frightened at the fire. Nothing stirred. I heard only the crackling of the flames and the sighs of a wounded man leaning against the wall of our stable. He had a ball in his loins, and leaned forward, supporting himself on his hands. He was a Croat. He looked at me with terrible, despairing eyes. A little further on, a horse, lying on his side, swung his head to and fro, on his long neck, like a pendulum. As I stood there, thinking that the French must be great brigands, to burn our houses without any reason, I heard a faint sound behind me. Turning round, I saw in the gloom of the shed under the straw falling from the beams, the half open door of the barn, and behind it the pale face and staring eyes

4   49

of our neighbor Spick. He put his head out softly, and listened; then, convinced that the Republicans had retreated, he rushed out, brandishing his axe like a madman, and crying:

"Where are they, those beggars? Where are they—let me exterminate them!"

"Ah," said I; "they're gone, but if you run, you can overtake them at the end of the village."

He gave me a sidelong glance, and seeing that I spoke innocently, left me, and ran to the fire. Other doors now opened, and men and women came out, looked around them, and raised their hands to heaven, crying:

"Curse them! Curse them!"

They all hastened with their buckets to extinguish the fire. The fountain was soon surrounded. They formed a line on both sides of the barricade, which extended to the houses that were in danger. Some soldiers standing on the roof, poured water upon the flames; but all they could do was to save the neighboring houses. Toward eleven o'clock a column of bluish fire rose toward the sky; among the vehicles that were piled up was found the *cantinière's* cart; its two casks of brandy had burst. Uncle Jacob was in the line, also, on the other side, under the guard of the Austrian sentinels; but he managed to escape while crossing a yard, and entered our house by the garden.

" Oh Lord," cried he, " Fritzel is saved! "

I saw by this how much he loved me. He kissed me, and asked:

" Where have you been, poor child? "

" At the window," said I.

He became very pale, and cried:

" Lisbeth! Lisbeth! "

But she did not answer, and we could not find her, although we went into all the rooms, and even looked under the beds. We thought she must have gone to some neighbor's house for safety. Meanwhile they had put out the fire, and suddenly we heard the Austrians cry outside:

" Room! room! fall back! "

And a regiment of Croats passed us like a thunderbolt. They rushed on in pursuit of the Republicans; but we learned the next day, that they had arrived too late; the enemy had gained the forest of Rothalps, which extended as far as the Pirmasens. Now we understood why they had barricaded the street and set fire to the houses. They wished to retard the pursuit of the cavalry, and thus showed their great experience in war.

From that moment until five in the evening two

Austrian brigades were defiling into the village under our windows; lancers, dragoons, hussars; then
cannon and army-wagons ; toward three o'clock,
the general-in-chief, in the midst of his officers,—
a large old man in a three-cornered hat, and long
white *Polonaise*,* so covered with lace and gold
embroidery that the Republican commander, in his
shabby hat and uniform, would have looked like
a simple corporal beside him. The burgomaster and
councillors of Anstatt, in cloth coats with large
sleeves, their heads uncovered, awaited him in the
square. He stopped there a few minutes, and looking at the dead bodies heaped up around the fountain, asked:

" How many of the French were here? "

" A battalion, your Excellency," replied the burgomaster, bent double.

The general said nothing, but raised his three-
cornered hat, and pursued his way.

Then the second brigade arrived; Tyrolese rifle-
men in front, in green coats, black hats, with turned-
up brims, and little Inspruck carbines; then another
troop of infantry in white coats, sky-blue breeches,
and great gaiters reaching to their knees; then the
heavy cavalry, men six feet high, encased in cui-

* Polish robe.

rasses, only the chin and long red moustache visible under the visor of the helmet; then came large ambulances, covered with gray linen, stretched over hoops, and behind them, the lame, the stragglers, and the cowards. The army surgeons made the tour of the square, raised the wounded, and placed them in the wagons, and one of their leaders, a little old man in a white wig, said to the burgomaster, pointing to those who remained:

" You will bury all those as soon as possible."

" Your orders shall be obeyed, sir," answered he, gravely.

At length the last wagons rolled away. It was about six o'clock. Night had come. Uncle Jacob and I stood in the doorway. Before us, near the fountain, all the dead lay in rows, with upturned faces, and staring eyes, white as wax, and bloodless. The women and children of the village walked around them. When the grave-digger, Jeffer, with his two sons, Karl and Ludwig, arrived with their pick-axes on their shoulders, the burgomaster said to them:

" Take twelve men with you, and dig a deep grave for all these bodies, in the meadow of the Wolfthal. Do you hear me? And all who have carts must lend them, with their horses; for it is a public service."

Jeffer bent his head, and went immediately to the meadow of the Wolfthal, with his two boys and the men whom he had chosen.

"Now, we must find Lisbeth," said my uncle.

We recommenced our search, going from garret to cellar, and at last, just as we were going to re-mount the stairs, we saw in the darkness, behind the barrel of sour-krout between the two air-holes, a bundle of linen, which my uncle began to shake. Lisbeth cried immediately in a pitiful voice—

"Don't kill me! In heaven's name have pity upon me!"

"Get up," said my uncle, kindly; "it is all over."

But she was still so much frightened that she could hardly put one foot before the other, and I had to lead her up stairs by the hand, like a child. Then finding herself again in the kitchen, she sat down by the hearth, and burst into tears, praying, and thanking God for having saved her;—which proves that the old cling to life quite as much as the young.

I shall never forget the hours of desolation which followed, and the constant calls upon my uncle from the unfortunates who claimed his care. Not a mo-ment passed but a woman or child ran into the house,

crying: "Doctor! come quickly; my husband—
my brother—my sister—are ill! "

One had been wounded, another had become
almost insane with fear; another, stretched out to
his full length, gave no sign of life. My uncle
could not be everywhere.

"You will find him at such a house," I would
say to these wretched ones; "make haste! "

And they would hasten away. It was very late,
nearly ten o'clock, when he at last returned. Lisbeth had recovered from her fright a little. She
had made the fire on the hearth, and laid the table,
as usual; but the plastering from the ceiling, the
pieces of window-glass and wood still covered the
floor. In the midst of it all, we seated ourselves
at the table, and ate in silence. From time to time,
my uncle raised his head, and looked out on the
square, at the torches moving around the dead, the
black carts stationed before the fountain, with their
little country ponies, the grave-diggers, the lookers
on,—all out in the darkness. He observed them
gravely, and suddenly, when we had nearly finished,
he said to me, stretching out his hand:

"Behold what war is, Fritzel;—look, and remember! Yes, this is war; death and destruc-
tion, fury and hatred, disregard of all human

feelings. When God strikes us with His curses, when he sends us pestilence and famine, these are at least inevitable scourges, decreed by His wisdom. But here it is man himself, who decrees misery to his kind, spreads his ravages far and wide, without pity. Yesterday, we were at peace; we asked nothing of anybody; we had done no harm; —and suddenly strange men came to strike, to ruin and destroy us. Ah, cursed be those whose ambitious spirit provokes such misfortunes! Let them be execrated through all ages! Fritzel, remember this; war is all that is most abominable on earth. Men who do not know, who have never seen each other, rush suddenly together, to tear each other to pieces. This alone would make us believe in God, for there must be an avenger of such iniquity."

My uncle spoke earnestly. He was much moved; and I listened with head bowed down, retaining every word and graving it upon my memory. As we sat thus, a kind of dispute arose outside in the square. We heard a dog growl, and our neighbor Spick say, angrily:

"Stop! stop! you beggar of a dog. I'll give you a blow with my pick-axe! He's an animal of the same species as his masters. They pay you with *assignats* * and bites; but I'm not the man to submit to that!"

The dog growled more fiercely. Other voices broke the silence of the night:

"It is very curious, though: see, he won't leave the woman. Perhaps she isn't quite dead."

My uncle rose hastily, and went out. I followed. Nothing could be more terrible than the sight of those dead bodies in the red reflection of the torches. There was no wind, but the flame swayed to and fro, and all those ghostly creatures with open eyes seemed to move.

"Not dead!" cried Spick. "Are you a fool, Jeffer? Do you think that you know more than the army surgeons? No, no, she's received her due. She's well served—she's the woman who paid for my brandy with paper. Go away from here, that I may kill the dog, and thus end the matter."

"What's going on here?" asked my uncle, in a loud voice. They all turned round and looked frightened. The grave-digger took off his hat, two or three others moved aside, and we saw on the steps of the fountain, the *cantinière* stretched out, white as snow, her beautiful black hair all unbound, in a pool of blood; her little cask still at

* The paper money of the French Republic.

her side, and her pale hands thrown to the right and left on the wet stones, over which the water flowed. Several corpses lay around her, and at her feet was the spaniel that I had seen in the morning with the little drummer,—the hair standing up on his back, his eyes flashing and lips trembling, as he looked at Spick, growling and shivering. Notwithstanding his great courage and his pick-axe, the innkeeper dared not approach, for it was easy to see that if he missed his blow the dog would leap at his throat.

" What is this?" repeated Uncle Jacob.

" Because the dog remains here," answered Spick, sneeringly, " they say the woman isn't dead."

" They are right," said my uncle, sharply. " Some animals have more mind and heart than some men. Take yourself away!"

He pushed him aside with his elbow, went to the woman, and bent over her. The dog, instead of springing upon him, seemed to grow quiet, and allowed him to do as he would. The others came near. My uncle knelt down, uncovered her bosom, and placed his hand on her heart. No one spoke; the silence was profound. It lasted nearly a minute, then Spick said:

" Ha! ha! Let them bury her. Isn't it so, doctor?"

MY UNCLE KNELT DOWN.

Uncle Jacob rose, frowning, and looked at the man sternly, from head to foot.

"Wretched man!" said he, "on account of a few pints of brandy, for which this poor woman paid you as well as she could, you now wish to see her dead, and perhaps buried alive!"

"Doctor!" cried the innkeeper, straightening himself with an arrogant air, "do you know that there are laws, and that"——

"Silence!" interrupted my uncle. "Your behavior is infamous!" Then turning to the others: "Jeffer, carry this woman into my house—she still lives."

He threw a last indignant look at Spick, while the grave-digger and his sons placed the *cantinière* on the litter. They went toward the house. The dog followed Uncle Jacob, pressing close to his legs. As to the innkeeper, we heard him say behind us, mockingly:

"The woman's dead! This doctor knows as much about it as my pick-axe. The woman's dead—it makes no difference whether she's buried to-day or to-morrow. We'll see which of us is right."

As we were crossing the square, I saw the mole-catcher and Koffel following us, which re-assured

me; for since night had come, a sort of terror had
seized me, especially when near the dead bodies,
and I was glad to have a good many people about.
The mole-catcher walked before the litter, holding
a large torch. Koffel kept near my uncle and looked
grave.

"These are terrible things, doctor," said he.

"Ah, is it you, Koffel? Yes, yes, the genius of
evil is in the air, the spirits of darkness are un-
chained."

We entered the little alley, which was filled with
rubbish. The mole-catcher stopped in the doorway to light Jeffer and his sons, who came forward
with heavy steps. We followed them into the room,
and raising his torch, he said, in a solemn tone:

"Where are the days of tranquillity, the moments of peace, repose and trust, after labor—
where are they, doctor? Ah, they have flown away
through all these openings!"

Then I noticed for the first time the desolate
look of our old room, with its broken windows,
whose shining fragments gleamed in the darkness.
I understood the mole-catcher's words, and thought
that we were indeed unfortunate.

"Jeffer, lay the woman on my bed," said my
uncle, sadly. "Our own miseries must not make

us forget those who are even more unhappy than we are." And turning to the mole-catcher: " You will stay and hold the light for me, and Koffel will help me."

The grave-digger and his sons having placed the litter on the floor, lifted the woman out, and put her upon the bed in the alcove. The mole-catcher held the torch, the reflections of which made his ruddy face look purple. Uncle Jacob gave some kreutzers to Jeffer, who went away with his boys. Old Lisbeth had come to see what was going on. She trembled and dared not approach the bed, and I heard her repeating the *Ave Maria* in a low tone. Her terror was beginning to infect me, when my uncle cried:

" Lisbeth, what are you thinking of? In heaven's name, are you crazy? Isn't this woman like all women, and haven't you helped me in my operations a hundred times? Come—come—folly has taken possession of you. Go heat some water, that's all the assistance I can hope for from you."

The dog was sitting in front of the alcove, looking, through his shaggy hair, at the woman stretched upon the bed, pale and motionless as a corpse.

" Fritzel," said my uncle, " close the shutters; we must have less air. And you, Koffel, make a fire in the stove, for we cannot expect to get any help from Lisbeth now. Ah, if amid so much wretchedness we still had the good sense to keep somewhat calm! But all must be in confusion. When the devil starts out, no one knows where he'll stop."

He spoke in a discouraged tone. I ran out to close the shutters, and heard him fasten them inside. Looking toward the fountain, I saw two more carts laden with the dead. I re-entered the house, shivering. Koffel had lighted the fire which crackled in the stove. My uncle opened his case of instruments on the table. The mole-catcher stood by, looking at the thousand shining little knives. Uncle Jacob took a probe and approached the bed, putting aside the curtains. The mole-catcher and Koffel followed. Curiosity impelled me to watch them. The candle lighted up the alcove; my uncle had cut open the *cantinière's* jacket. Koffel, with a large sponge, bathed her breast, which was covered with dark blood. The dog watched him without stirring. Lisbeth also had returned. She held my hand, and muttered some prayer. No one spoke in the alcove, and my uncle, hearing the old servant, cried, angrily:

"Will you be quiet, foolish woman! Come mole-catcher, come, raise her arm."

" A beautiful creature," said the mole-catcher, " still very young."

" How pale she is! " said Koffel.

I went nearer and saw her lying there, white as snow, her head thrown back, and her black hair falling around her. The mole-catcher held up her arm, and beneath it, between the breast and the arm-pit, appeared a bluish opening from which flowed some drops of blood. Uncle Jacob, his lips compressed, probed this wound; the probe would not go in. I became so interested, never having seen anything of the kind, that my whole soul was in that alcove, and I heard my uncle murmur—

" It is strange! "

At that moment the woman breathed a long sigh, and the dog, who had been quiet until then, began to cry in a voice as lamentable and gentle as a human being's. It made my hair stand on end.

" Be silent! " cried the mole-catcher.

The dog was silent, and my uncle said:

" Raise the arm again, mole-catcher. Koffel, come here and support the body."

Koffel went behind the bed, and raised the woman by the shoulders. The probe immediately went in very far. She groaned, and the dog growled.

" There," cried my uncle, " she is saved. Hold,

Koffel, see: the ball has glanced along the ribs, it is here, under the shoulder. Do you feel it?"

"Very plainly."

Uncle Jacob went out, and seeing me behind the curtain, cried:

"What are you doing here?"

"I'm looking."

"Good, now, he's looking! Everything goes wrong."

He took a knife from the table and went back.

The dog watched me with his shining eyes, which disturbed me. Suddenly the woman uttered a cry, and my uncle exclaimed, joyfully:

"See! it is a pistol-ball. The poor creature has lost a great deal of blood, but she will recover."

"She must have received that during the great charge of the lancers," said Koffel. "I was at old Kræmer's, on the first floor, cleaning his clock, and I saw that they fired as they came in."

"It's possible," answered my uncle, who now for the first time thought of looking at the woman's face.

He took the candle from the mole-catcher, and standing behind the bed, looked dreamily for some seconds at the unfortunate creature.

FOR SEVERAL MOMENTS HE CONTEMPLATED THIS UNFORTUNATE
CREATURE.

" Yes," he said, " she is a beautiful woman, and has a noble head. How sad that such creatures should follow the army. How much better would it be to see them in the bosom of an honest family, surrounded by lovely children, beside an honest man whose happiness they would make. What a shame! After all, though, it is the will of God."

He went out, calling Lisbeth.

" Get some of your clothes for this woman, and put them on her," he said. " Mole-catcher, Koffel, come; we will have a glass of wine, for this has been a hard day for us."

He went down into the cellar, and returned just as the old servant came in with the garments. Lisbeth, seeing that the *cantinière* was not dead, had taken courage; she went into the alcove and drew the curtains, while my uncle uncorked the bottle and went to the side-board for glasses. The mole-catcher and Koffel seemed content. I, too, drew near the table, which was still laid, and we finished our supper. The dog watched us at a distance. My uncle threw him some pieces of bread, but he would not eat them. The church-clock struck one.

" It is half-past twelve," said Koffel.

" No," replied the mole-catcher, " it is one o'clock. I think it is time for us to go to bed."

5

Lisbeth came out from the alcove, and we all went in to see the *cantinière*. She seemed to sleep. The dog placed his fore paws on the edge of the bed, and looked at her also. Uncle Jacob patted his head, saying:

" Don't be afraid; she will get well, I promise thee! "

The poor animal seemed to understand, and whined softly. Then we went out. My uncle lighted Koffel and the mole-catcher to the door, and then said to us:

" Go to bed, now, it's time."

" And you, doctor? " asked the old servant.

" I shall watch—this woman's in danger, and they may also want me in the village."

He put a log on the fire, and threw himself back on the arm-chair, twisting a piece of paper to light his pipe. Lisbeth and I went up to our rooms, but it was very late before I could get to sleep, despite my great fatigue; for every half-hour the rumbling of carts and the reflection of torches on the windows, told me that the dead were still passing. At length, at daybreak, all the noises ceased, and I slept soundly.

V

WHAT a sight the village was the next day when each one was trying to find out what remained, and what he had lost. They found that a great number of Republicans, lancers, and Croats had entered the houses through the back doors, and ransacked them. Then there was general indignation, and I felt that the mole-catcher was right in saying:

"The days of peace and quiet have flown away through these openings."

All the doors and windows were thrown open so the havoc might be seen; the street was filled with furniture, vehicles, cattle, and men who were exclaiming,

"Ah, the beggars! Ah, the robbers! They've taken everything!"

One was looking for his ducks, another for his chickens, another found under his bed a pair of old shoes instead of his boots, a fourth, finding his chimney-place empty, where sausages and pieces of bacon had hung the morning before, went into a terrible passion; the women raised their hands to heaven in despair, and the girls seemed stupefied. Butter, eggs, tobacco, potatoes, even linen—had all been stolen. The more they looked, the more they missed. The greatest rage was felt against the Croats, for after the general had passed, they, no longer fearing that they might be complained of, had rushed into the houses like a band of famished wolves, and God knows how much had been given them to induce them to go, without reckoning what they had taken.

It is very unfortunate that old Germany has soldiers from whom she has more to fear than from the French. The Lord preserve us from ever again needing their aid. We children, Hans Aden, Frantz Sépel, Nickel, Johann, and I, went from door to door, looking at the broken tiles and shutters, and unroofed sheds, and picking up scraps, papers of cartridges, and balls flattened against the walls. We enjoyed these treasures so much, that we did not think of returning home before nightfall. Toward two o'clock we met Zaphéri Schmouck, the basket-maker's son, who held up his red head, and seemed prouder than usual. He had something hidden under his blouse, and when we asked,

" What have you got there? " he showed us the end of a great horse-pistol.

Then we all followed him.

He marched in the midst of us like a general; we said to every boy we met, " He's got a pistol," and the new-comer would join the troop.

We would not have left Schmouck for an empire. It seemed to us that the glory of his pistol was reflected upon us.

Such are children, and such are men!

Each boasted of the dangers he had incurred during the great battle.

" I heard the balls whistle," said Frantz Sépel, " two of them came into our kitchen."

" I saw the general of the lancers galloping, in his red cap," cried Hans Aden, " that was much more terrible than hearing the balls whistle."

What elated me most was that the Republican commander had given me the cake, saying: " Eat this boldly! " I thought myself worthy of having a pistol, like Zaphéri;—but nobody would believe me.

As we passed the steps of the Town Hall Schmouck cried:

" Come and see! "

We mounted the grand staircase behind him, and stopping before the door of the council-chamber, which was pierced by a square opening as large as one's hand, he said:

" Look—the dead men's clothes are there. Jeffer
and the burgomaster brought them in a cart, this
morning."

We remained more than an hour looking at these
clothes, climbing on each other's shoulders, and
whispering:

" Let me look now, Hans Aden—it's my turn,"
etc.

The clothes were piled up in the middle of the
large, deserted room, under the dim light of two
high grated windows. There were the Republican
hats and lancers' caps, belts and pouches, blue coats,
and red cloaks, sabres, and pistols. The guns were
placed against the walls on the right, and further
on we saw a row of lances.

The sight of them gave me a chill, and I have
never forgotten them.

At the end of an hour, when night came, one of
the boys suddenly became frightened, and ran down
the stairs, crying in a loud voice:

" Here they are! "

Then all the party rushed down the steps, falling
over each other in the darkness. It is a wonder that
we did not break our necks, so great was our terror.
I was the last; and although my heart beat vio-
lently, I turned at the foot of the stairs, to look

back. It was nearly dark in the vestibule; through
a little window on the right, a faint ray of light fell
on the dark steps. Not a sound disturbed the silence under the sombre vault. The cries in the
street died away in the distance. I began to fear
that my uncle would be anxious about me, and went
home alone, not without looking around again; for
it seemed to me that stealthy steps were following
me, and I dared not run.

I stopped before the inn of the Two Keys, whose
windows shone in the darkness of the night. The
noise of the drinkers reassured me. I looked
through the little opening in the door, into the large
room, where there was the hum of many voices, and
saw Koffel, the mole-catcher, M. Richter, and many
others seated at the deal tables, bending over pitch-
ers and goblets. The angular figure of M. Richter,
in his hunting-jacket and leather cap, was ges-
ticulating, under the hanging lamp, in the gray
smoke.

"Behold these famous Republicans," said he,
"these terrible men who are going to upset the
world. The glorious shadow of the Field Marshal Wurmser is sufficient to scatter them. You've
seen them turn their backs, and stretch their legs!
How many times have I told you that their great

enterprise would end in an explosion? Mole-catcher, Koffel, didn't I say so?"

"Yes, you said so," replied the mole-catcher, "but that's no reason why you should talk so loud. Come, M. Richter, sit down and order a bottle of wine; Koffel and I've paid for ours. That's the principal thing."

M. Richter sat down, and I went home. It was about half-past seven o'clock. The passage was swept, and the window-panes reset. I went at once to the kitchen, and Lisbeth seeing me, cried:

"Oh, here he is." She opened the door and said, in a lower tone, "Doctor, the child's come!"

"Very well," said my uncle, who was seated at the table, "let him come in."

I was beginning to speak loud.

"Hush!" said he, pointing to the alcove, "sit down; you must have a good appetite."

"Yes, uncle."

"Where do you come from?"

"I've been to see the village."

"Very well, Fritzel; you've made me uneasy, but I'm glad you've witnessed these horrors."

Lisbeth brought me a good plate of soup, and while I ate, he added—

" Now, you know what war is. Remember these things, Fritzel, to curse them. It is a good lesson. What we see in our youth, remains with us all our lives."

He spoke to himself rather than to me;—I was too much occupied with my supper to attend. After soup, Lisbeth gave me meat and vegetables; but just as I was taking my fork, I saw a motionless creature sitting near me on the floor, watching me. This startled me.

" Don't be afraid, Fritzel," said my uncle, smiling.

I looked again and saw that it was the *cantinière's* dog. He was sitting gravely, with upturned nose and hanging ears, observing me attentively.

" Give him some of your supper, and you will soon be good friends."

He called the dog, who came and seated himself near his chair, seeming well pleased with the little pats my uncle gave him on the head. He licked my plate clean, then looked at me again seriously. Supper was nearly over and I was just going to rise from the table, when a confused muttering was heard in the alcove. My uncle listened ; the woman was speaking extremely fast and low. Those confused, mysterious words, in the midst of the silence, moved me more than all the rest. I felt that I turned pale. Uncle Jacob, his head bent forward, looked at me, but his thoughts were elsewhere ; he was listening. Among the many words she uttered, a few were very distinct.

" My father—Jean—killed—all—all—my country ! "

I saw that my uncle was much troubled ; his lips trembled. He took the lamp and approached the bed. Lisbeth entered, to clear the table. He turned to her and said :

" See, fever has set in," and he drew aside the curtains. She followed. I did not move from my chair. I was no longer hungry. The woman was silent. I saw my uncle's and Lisbeth's shadows on the curtains. He held the woman's arm. The dog was in the alcove with them. I was alone in the dark room, and felt afraid. The *cantinière* spoke again more loudly ; then the room seemed to grow darker, and I drew near the light. But at that moment there was a struggle ; Lisbeth, who was holding the lamp, recoiled, and the woman, very pale, with wide open eyes, half rose, crying :

" Jean—Jean—take care—I'm coming ! " Then she uttered a great cry—" Long live the Republic!" and fell back.

My uncle came out, exclaiming in great agitation :

" Lisbeth, quick, quick, go upstairs in the closet —the gray vial with a glass stopper—hurry! "

He re-entered the alcove. Lisbeth ran upstairs; I held fast to my uncle's coat. The dog growled ; the woman was stretched out as if dead. Lisbeth returned with the vial. Uncle Jacob looked at it, and said, quickly,

" That's it—a spoon ! "

I ran to get my spoon. He wiped it, poured a few drops into it, and raising the woman's head made her swallow them, saying, with extreme gentleness,

" Come, come, courage, my child—courage ! "

I had never heard him speak in a voice so sweet, so tender—it touched my heart. The *cantinière* sighed gently. My uncle laid her back upon the bed, raising her pillow. Then he came out, looking very pale, and said to us :

" Go to bed, leave me—I'm going to watch."

" But, doctor," said Lisbeth, " last night "——

" Go to bed," repeated he, impatiently. " I haven't time to listen to your babbling. For heaven's sake leave me in peace—this may become serious ! "

We felt that he must be obeyed.

As we went upstairs, Lisbeth said,

"Did you see that unhappy creature, Fritzel? Perhaps she's going to die. Yet she is still thinking of that devilish Republic! Those people are real savages. All that we can do is to pray to God to pardon them."

Then she began to pray. I knew not what to think of all this, but after having run about so much, and wallowed in dirt, once in bed I slept so soundly that not even the return of the Republicans themselves, with all their platoons and battalion-firing, would have waked me before ten the next morning.

VI.

THE day after the departure of the Republicans, everybody in the village knew that there was a French woman at Uncle Jacob's house, who had received a pistol-shot, and was recovering very slowly. But the roofs of the houses, the doors and windows must be repaired, and each had enough business of his own to attend to, without troubling himself about the affairs of others, and it was not until the third day, when things were nearly all put in order again, that people began to think about the woman. Then Joseph Spick spread the news that the French woman had become raving, and cried, " Long live the Republic ! " in a terrible manner.

The scoundrel stood in the doorway of his inn, his arms crossed, leaning against the wall, pretending to smoke his pipe, and saying to the passers-by :

" Nickel—Yokel—listen !—listen how she screams ! Isn't it abominable? Ought we to allow this? "

Uncle Jacob, the best man in the world, was so in-

dignant with Spick, that I heard him say several
times, that he deserved to be hung.   Unhappily, we
could not deny that the *cantinière* spoke of France,
of the Republic, and other things contrary to good
order.   These ideas always returned to her mind,
and we were the more embarrassed because all the
gossips, all the old Salomes of the village came in
procession to our house ; one with her broom under
her arm, and petticoat tucked up,—another with her
knitting-needles in her hair, and cap awry ; a third
bringing her spinning-wheel, with a sentimental air,
as if to spin in the chimney-corner.   This one came
to borrow a gridiron, that one to buy a pot of curdled
milk, or to ask for a little yeast, to make bread.
What a shame !   Our passage was two inches deep
in mud from their wooden shoes.   And to hear them
chatter while Lisbeth washed her dishes, or watched
her pots ; to see them come in, courtesying, and
playing the agreeable !

"Ah ! good day, M'lle Lisbeth.   How long it is
since I've seen you ! "

"Ah, it's M'lle Oursoula !   God of heaven ! how
glad I am to see you.   Do sit down, M'lle Oursoula ! "

"Oh, you're too good, too good !   M'lle Lisbeth !
What beautiful weather, this morning ! "

" Yes, M'lle Oursoula—very fine weather—delicious weather for rheumatism."

" Delicious for colds, also."

" Ah, yes ! and for all kinds of sickness. How is *monsieur le curé's* rheumatism, M'lle Oursoula? "

" Oh, Lord ! How should it be? Sometimes on one side—sometimes on the other. Yesterday in the shoulder—to-day in the back. So it moves about. Always suffering, always suffering ! "

" Ah, I'm sorry to hear it—very sorry ! "

" But *apropos*, M'lle Lisbeth, you'll call me very curious—they are talking about it all over the village ; is your French lady still ill? "

" Ah, M'lle Oursoula, don't speak of it ; we've had such a night—such a night ! "

" Is it possible? That poor lady is no better? What do I hear? "

And they would clasp their hands, and bend forward with an air of great commiseration, rolling their eyes, and shaking their heads.

The first two days, my uncle, thinking this would end when people's curiosity was gratified, said nothing. But seeing that it still continued, he entered the kitchen abruptly, one fine morning, when his patient had a great deal of fever and said to the old women, angrily :

" What do you come here for?   Why don't you
stay at home?   Have you no work in your houses?
You ought to be ashamed to pass your lives in
chattering like old magpies, and giving yourselves
the airs of great ladies, when you are nothing
but servants.   It is ridiculous, and I'm very tired
of it! "

" But," answered one, " I came to buy a pot of
milk."

" Does it take two hours to buy a pot of milk? "
replied he, really angry.   " Lisbeth, give her the
pot of milk, and let her go with the others.   I'm
tired of all this.   I shall allow no one to come here
to spy, and take false news from my house to spread
over the country.   Go, and don't come here again."

The gossips went off quite ashamed.

That day my uncle had a great discussion.   M.
Richter ventured to say to him that he was wrong
to interest himself so much in strangers, who came
into the country to pillage, and above all in this
woman, who could not be of much account, as she
had followed the soldiers.   He listened coldly, and
answered :

" M. Richter, when I do a humane act, I do not
ask the person, ' From what country are you? Have
you the same belief as I?   Are you rich or poor?

Can you pay me for what I have done for you?' I follow the impulse of my heart, and the rest matters little. Whether this woman be French or German, whether she has Republican ideas or not, whether she has followed the soldiers of her own accord, or been forced to do so by necessity, does not trouble me. I saw that she was dying ; my duty was to save her life. And now my duty is, with the help of God, to go on with what I have undertaken. As to you, M. Richter, I know you are an egotist ; you do not love your fellow-creatures. Instead of rendering them a service, you seek to gain some personal advantage from them. This is the foundation of your opinion on all matters. And as such opinions make me angry, I beg that you will not enter my house again."

He opened the door, and as M. Richter wished to reply, without listening to him, he politely took him by the arm, and put him out. The mole-catcher, Koffel, and I were present, and Uncle Jacob's firmness on this occasion astonished us ; we had never seen him more calm and resolute. He only kept the mole-catcher and Koffel for his friends. Each in turn watched with the patient, which did not prevent them from attending to their business during the day.

6

From that time tranquillity was re-established in our house.

One morning, on awaking, I found that winter had come. Its white light filled my little room. Great snow-flakes were falling from the sky in myriads—whirling against my window-panes. All was still outside ; not a soul was in the street ; everybody's doors were closed ; the chickens were quiet ; the dogs looked out from their kennels, and in the neighboring thickets the poor green-finches, shivering under their ruffled feathers, uttered that plaintive cry of distress which lasts until spring. I, with my elbow on my pillow, and my eyes dazzled, looked at the snow piled up on the edge of the little windows, and pictured to myself past winters—the light from our great stove in the evenings, dancing on the floor, the mole-catcher, Koffel, and my uncle bending over it, smoking their pipes and talking of unimportant matters. I heard Lisbeth's wheel buzzing in the silence like the downy wings of a moth, and her foot keeping time to the song that the green log was singing on the hearth. Without, I pictured to myself the slides on the river, the sleighing parties, the battle with snow-balls, the shouts of laughter, the broken window-panes, the old grandmother calling after us, while the band scampered away.

All this came into my mind in a moment, and half sad, half glad, I said to myself, "It's winter." Then thinking it would be pleasant to be sitting in front of the fire, eating some of Lisbeth's good porridge, I sprang from my bed, and dressed myself quickly, feeling very chilly. Without taking time to put on both sleeves of my jacket, I went rolling downstairs like a ball. Lisbeth was sweeping the yard. The kitchen door was open, but despite the beautiful fire which danced around the pots, I hurried into the sitting-room. Uncle Jacob had just returned from a visit. His great riding-coat lined with foxes' fur, and his otter-skin cap, hung on the wall, and his large boots were near the stove. He was taking a glass of *kirschenwasser*,* with the mole-catcher, who had been watching that night. Both seemed in good spirits.

"So, mole-catcher," said my uncle, "the night has passed well?"

"Very well, doctor; we've all slept; the woman in her bed, I in the arm-chair, and the dog behind the curtain. Nobody has stirred. This morning, on opening the window, I saw the country as white as Hans Wurst, when he comes out of his bag of flour ; all had been done without a sound.

* Cherry-brandy.

As I opened the window, you were coming up the street, and I wanted to call out good morning, but the woman was still asleep, and I didn't want to wake her."

" Well, well, you did right.   To your health, mole-catcher."

" To yours, doctor."

They drained their little glasses at a draught, and put them on the table, smiling.

" All goes well," said Uncle Jacob ; " the wound is closing ; the fever diminishes, but strength is still wanting ; the poor thing has lost too much blood. But at last, at last, that will come right."

I sat down near the stove.   The dog came from the alcove, and began to caress my uncle, who said, looking at him :

" What a good animal !   See, mole-catcher, wouldn't you say that he understands us?   Doesn't he seem more joyous this morning?   I cannot but believe that these animals understand some things very well ; if they have less judgment than we, they often have more heart."

" That's true," said the mole-catcher.   " For my part, all the time the fever lasted, I would look at the dog and think ' He's sad ; that's a bad sign. He's gay ; that's a good sign ! '   On my honor, I agree with you, doctor. I have great confidence in the understanding of animals."

"Come, mole-catcher, take another little glass, it's cold out of doors, and the old *kirschenwasser* warms you like a ray of sunlight." He opened the side-board, took out a loaf of bread and two knives, and said, "Let us have a crust."

The mole-catcher nodded assent. My uncle, perceiving me, said, smilingly :

"Well, Fritzel, snow-balls and slides have come again. Doesn't that please you?"

"Yes, uncle."

"Yes, yes, amuse yourself. One is never happier than at your age, my boy. But above all, don't make your snow-balls too hard. Those who make them too hard don't want to amuse themselves, they want to do harm ; they're bad boys."

"Ah, doctor," said the mole-catcher, laughing, "I always made my balls too hard."

"And see how wrong you were ; that proves that there was a spice of malice in your nature. Happily reason has conquered that. I'm sure you repent of having made your balls too hard."

"Oh, yes," said the mole-catcher, not knowing what to reply ; "although the rest made theirs too hard, too."

" We should never trouble ourselves about others. We must do what kindness commands. All men are naturally good and just ; but bad example leads them astray."

While we were talking, some words were heard in the alcove. We all became silent, and listened.

" That, mole-catcher, is not the voice of delirium," said Uncle Jacob. " It's a weak but natural voice."

He rose and drew aside the curtains. The mole-catcher and I stood behind him, stretching forward our heads. The woman, very pale and thin, seemed to be asleep ; we could hardly hear her breathe. But in a moment she opened her eyes, and looked from one to another in astonishment, then around the alcove, then at the windows white with snow, at the chest of drawers, the old clock, and at the dog, who stood with his paws on the edge of the bed. At length she closed her eyes, and my uncle said, in a very low tone :

" She has come to herself."

" Yes," said the mole-catcher, " she has seen us; she doesn't know us, and now she's thinking of what she has just seen."

We were going to withdraw, when she re-opened

her eyes, and made an effort to speak.   But Uncle
Jacob, raising his voice, said, kindly :

"Don't agitate yourself, madame; be calm; have
no uneasiness.   You are with those who will let you
want for nothing.   You've been ill, but you're getting better.   But I beg you to have ·confidence—
you're among friends—true friends."

She looked at him with her large black eyes, while
he spoke.   We could see that she understood him.
But notwithstanding his advice, she tried to speak
again, and said in a low voice :

"The drummer—the little drummer."

My uncle, looking at the mole-catcher, asked :

"Do you understand her?"

And the mole-catcher, putting his hand to his
head, answered :

"A remnant of fever, doctor—a little remnant—
it'll pass off."

But the woman in a loud voice repeated—

"Jean—the little drummer."

I was standing on tip-toe, very attentive, and it
suddenly occurred to me that she was speaking of
the little drummer whom I had seen lying in our
shed, the day of the great battle.   I remembered
how she watched him from the window, as she
mended his little pantaloons, and said :

"Uncle, perhaps she is speaking of the little drummer who was with the Republicans."

The poor woman at once tried to turn toward me.

"Yes, yes!" cried she. "Jean—my brother!"

"Be quiet, madame," said my uncle. "Don't move; your wound might re-open. Mole-catcher, bring a chair." And taking me under the arms, he placed me on the chair before her, saying, ' Tell madame what you know, Fritzel. Do you remember the little drummer?"

"Oh, yes! the morning of the battle he was lying under our shed; the dog was at his feet. He was asleep. I remember him well!" answered I, much disturbed, for she was looking at me as if she would search my very soul—just as she had looked at Uncle Jacob.

"And then, Fritzel?"

"Then he was with the other drummers in the midst of the battalion, when the Croats came. And at last, when they had set the street on fire, and the Republicans were leaving, I saw him in the rear."

"Wounded?" asked the woman, in a voice so faint that we could hardly hear it.

"Oh, no! he had his drum on his shoulder, and was crying as he marched, and a larger boy was saying to him, ' Courage, little Jean,—courage!' but he didn't seem to hear him—his cheeks were wet with tears."

" You are sure you saw him go away with them, Fritzel? " asked my uncle.

" Yes, uncle ; he made me sorry, and I watched him to the end of the village."

The *cantinière* closed her eyes, and sobbed quietly. Tears flowed down her face, one ofter another, in silence. It was very sad, and uncle said, softly :

" Get down, Fritzel ; we must let her cry without hindrance."

But as I was getting down, she stretched out her hand, and drew me to her, murmuring something. Uncle Jacob understood her, and asked :

" Do you wish to kiss the child? "

" Yes."

He held me toward her. She kissed me, sobbing. Then I too began to cry.

" Well, well ! " said my uncle. " You must be calm now, madame ; you must try to sleep if you would get well. You'll see your little brother again. Courage ! "

He took me out, and closed the curtains. The mole-catcher was walking up and down the room with long strides. His face was red, and he said :

" That's a good woman, doctor—an honest wom-

an—let her be a Republican, or what you will
They who think the contrary are no better than
scoundrels ! "

" Yes, she has a generous nature ; I knew it at
once by her face. It is fortunate that Fritzel re-
members the child. The poor woman was very
anxious. I understand now why the name of
Jean constantly recurred in her delirium. It is all
right, mole-catcher, it is all right—tears will soothe
her."

They went out together. I heard them still talking about her outside the door. And as I sat near
the stove, wiping my eyes on my sleeve, I suddenly
saw the dog near me, looking at me with great gentleness. He put his paw on my knee, and began to
caress me. For the first time I took his great
shaggy head between my hands without fear. It
seemed as if we had been friends for a long time,
and that I had never been afraid of him. Raising
my eyes, I saw Uncle Jacob, who had just come in,
and was watching me, smiling.

" You see, Fritzel, that the poor animal loves you.
He'll follow you now, for he's found out that you
have a kind heart."

And so it was ; from that day the dog no longer
refused to accompany me ; on the contrary, he fol-

lowed me gravely all over the village, which made me prouder than Zaphéri Schmouck with his lancers' pistol. He would sit near my chair, to eat from my plate, and do whatever I wished.

VII

THE snow continued to fall that day and the following night. Every one thought that the mountain roads would be blocked up, and that we should
see no more of the lancers nor the Republicans ; but
a little incident happened which served to show the
sad consequences of war, and to make men reflect
on the mishaps of this world.

It was the day after that on which our patient had
recovered her reason, between eight and nine in the
morning. The kitchen door was open so that the
stove might warm the sitting-room. I was standing by Lisbeth, who was churning butter near the
hearth. Turning my head a little I could see my
uncle sitting by the window, which was white with
snow, reading the almanac and smiling occasionally.

The dog Scipio was near me, grave and motionless, and as I every minute tasted the cream, which
was coming out of the churn, he gaped in a melancholy manner.

"But Fritzel," said Lisbeth, "what are you

thinking of? If you eat all the cream, we'll have no more butter."

The clock ticked slowly in the sitting-room ; out-of-doors the silence was perfect.

This lasted for half an hour, and Lisbeth had just put the fresh butter on a plate, when voices were heard in the street ; the gate opened, and feet covered with snow were stamped on the stones of the court. My uncle hung the almanac on the wall and looked toward the door, through which the burgomaster, Meyer, came in, with his cap of curled wool, with two tassels, drawn over his ears, the collar of his great coat white with frost, and his hands enclosed in rabbit-skin mittens which reached to his elbows.

" Good-day, doctor, good-day," said the large man. " I come at a snowy time. But what of that? It is necessary, it is necessary."

Then shaking his mittens, which hung from his neck by a string, he took off his cap and continued:

" A poor devil, doctor, is lying in Réebock's wood-house behind a heap of fagots. He's a soldier, or rather a corporal, or a captain. I don't know exactly which. He must have crept in there to die quietly, during the fight. It will be necessary to hold an inquest. I can't certify of what the man died—that's not part of my office."

" Well, burgomaster," said Uncle Jacob, rising, " I will go : but there must be one more witness."

" Michel Furst is outside, waiting at the gate. What a snow ! what a snow ! up to one's knees, doctor. It will be good for the crops, and for his majesty's armies, who will go into quarters—God bless them ! I would rather they should go to Kaiserslautern than come here; one never has a better friend than himself."

While the burgomaster indulged in these reflections, my uncle was putting on his boots, great coat, and otter-skin cap. Then he said :

" I am ready."

They went out, and despite the entreaties of Lisbeth, who wanted to keep me in, I hurried out, and followed them. I was seized with a curiosity to see the soldier.

Uncle Jacob, the burgomaster, and Furst, were the only persons in the deserted streets ; but as they walked along, faces appeared at the windows and doors were heard opening in the distance. People seeing the burgomaster, the doctor, and the *garde-champêtre** thought something *extraordinary* must

* An officer who has charge of the fields.

have happened, and several even came out, but, not finding out anything, went in again immediately.

Arriving at Réebock's house, one of the oldest in the village, with barn, stables, and shed in the fields behind, and thatched cow-houses with mouldy roofs on the right,—the burgomaster, Furst, and my uncle, entered the little gloomy passage paved with broken flag-stones.

I followed unperceived.

Old Réebock, who had seen them pass his windows, opened the door of the sitting-room, which was as full of smoke as a steam-bath, where the old grandmother, her two sons, and two daughters-in-law sat.

Their dog, with long gray hair and tail dragging on the ground, came out, also, and smelt Scipio, who followed me, holding himself proudly while the other walked around him, trying to make his acquaintance.

" I'll show you the way," said old Réebock— " it's there—inside—behind the barn."

" No, stay here, Father Réebock," said Uncle Jacob, " it's chilly, and you are old—your son will show us the way."

But the son, after discovering the soldier, had ran away.

The old man went before ; we followed in file. It was very dark in the passage. In passing we saw the cow-house lighted by a pane of glass in the roof, five goats with full udders, who looked at us with their golden brown eyes, and two kids who began to cry in a shrill, plaintive voice ; then the stable ; two oxen and the cow, with their worm-eaten racks and litter of dead leaves.

The animals turned quietly round. We walked along the wall : something rolled under my feet. It was a rabbit which disappeared under the manger. Scipio did not stir.

Then we came to the barn, low, filled with hay and straw to the roof. Inside we saw a window of bluish glass opening in the garden ; the light from it fell upon a great pile of logs and some fagots heaped against the wall ; below all was dark.

Strange to say, in the window were a cock and two or three hens, their heads under their wings, who stood out black against the light. I could not see much at first, on account of the gloom. We all stopped. The hens gave a low cackle.

" Perhaps I should have lighted the lantern," said old Réebock : " we can't see very well."

As he spoke, I saw to the right of the window, against the wall, between two fagots, a large red cloak : then looking closer, a dark head and yellow-ish mustache; the cock jumped down from the window and made it lighter.

I was seized with fear. Had I not felt Scipio against my leg, I should have run away.

" I see," said my uncle, " I see ! " And he ap-proached, saying : " It is a Croat. Let us see— Furst, we must draw him forward a little."

But neither Furst nor the burgomaster moved.

My uncle drew the man by the leg, so that the light fell upon him. He had a red head, sunken eyes, pinched nose, compressed lips, and a reddish tuft on his chin. Uncle Jacob unbuckled his cloak, throwing the folds over the wood, and we saw that the Croat held a sabre with a long blue curved blade. On his left side a large black spot showed that he had bled there. My uncle unbuttoned his vest and said:

" He died of a bayonet-stroke, doubtless during the last encounter. He must have withdrawn from the contest. Father Réebock, what astonishes me, is that he did not knock at your door, and that he came so far to die."

" We were all hidden in the cellar," said the old man ; " the door of the room was shut. We heard some one running in the passage, but there was so much noise outside. I believe the poor man wanted

7

to escape through the house ; unfortunately there is no back door. A Republican must have followed him like a wild beast as far as the barn. We've seen no blood in the passage ; it is here in the darkness that they must have fought, and the Frenchman, after giving him this bad blow, must have gone quietly away. This is what I think ; otherwise we should have found blood somewhere. But no one has seen any, either in the stable or the cow-house. It was not till this morning, when we needed some large wood for the stove, that Sépel, going into the woodhouse, discovered the unfortunate man."

As we listened to this explanation, we pictured to ourselves the Republican with his great queue, like a black sausage, and his large pointed hat, pursuing the Croat in the darkness, and it made one tremble.

" Yes," said Uncle Jacob, rising, and looking at the burgomaster, sadly, " that's the way it must have happened."

All became thoughtful. The silence near the dead body chilled me.

" Now the inquest is over," said my uncle, in a moment, " we can go." Then, be-thinking himself, " Perhaps there may be some means of finding out who this man is."

He knelt again, put his hand into the man's

pocket, and drew out some papers. Then he pulled a little copper chain that crossed his breast, and drew a large silver watch from the fob of his pantaloons.

" Take the watch," he said to the burgomaster. " I'll keep the papers until I've written the certificate."

" Keep everything, doctor," said the burgomaster. " I don't like to carry into my house a watch which has already marked the death of one of God's creatures—no, keep everything. Later, we'll talk of this again. Now, let us go."

" Yes, and you may send Jeffer."

Then my uncle, perceiving me, said :

" You here, Fritzel? Must you then see everything? "

He made no other reproach, and we went home together. The burgomaster and Furst went to their homes. As we walked along, Uncle Jacob read the Croat's papers. Opening the door of our room, we saw that the woman had just taken some broth ; the curtains were still open and the plate on the table.

" Well, madame," said my uncle, smiling, " you're getting better."

She had turned and was looking at him gratefully with her large black eyes.

" Yes, doctor, you have saved me. I feel that I'm recovering." Then, in a second, she added in a tone full of compassion—" You have just found another unfortunate victim of war."

My uncle knew then that she had overheard the conversation when the burgomaster came for him half an hour before.

" It is true, it is true, madame ; another unfortunate creature who will never more see his home ; another poor mother who will never again embrace her son."

She seemed moved, and asked in a low voice :

" Is it one of our men? "

" No, madame ; he is a Croat. I have just been reading a letter that his mother wrote him three weeks ago. The poor woman begs him not to forget his prayers night and morning, and to do right. She speaks to him with tenderness, as if he were a child. Yet he was an old soldier ; but doubtless she saw him still fresh and fair as on the day when, for the last time, she embraced him, sobbing."

My uncle's voice, as he said this, was very touching. He looked at the woman, who also seemed much moved.

" Yes, you are right," said she, " it must be dreadful to know that a child will never come back

again.   I, at least, have the consolation of no longer
causing such suffering to those who loved me."

She turned away her head, and my uncle, who had
become very grave, asked her :

"Yet you are not alone in the world?"

"I have neither father nor mother," said she,
sadly ; "my father was commander of the battalion
that you saw.   I had three brothers.   We all came
away together in '92 from Fénétrange in Lorraine.
Three are now dead ; my father and two eldest
brothers ; only I, and Jean the little drummer, are
left."   As she said this, she seemed ready to burst
into tears.   Uncle Jacob, his head bent forward, his
arms crossed on his back, walked up and down the
room.   Again all was silent.   Suddenly the French
woman said : "I have something to ask you, doctor."

"What, madame?"

"Write to the mother of the unfortunate Croat.
It is terrible, no doubt, to hear of the death of a son,
but to be always expecting him, to hope for years
that he will return, and yet never to see him—even
at one's last hour, that must be more cruel still."

She ceased, and my uncle said, thoughtfully :

"Yes, yes, it is a good thought.   Fritzel, bring
the ink and paper.   What a terrible thing, my God!

To think that writing such news to a mother should be considered a good deed.   Oh war ! war ! "

He sat down and began to write.   Lisbeth came in to lay the cloth.   She put the plates and loaf on the side-board.   Twelve o'clock struck.   The *cantinière* seemed to be sleeping.   Uncle Jacob finished his letter, folded, sealed, and addressed it, and said to me :

" Go, Fritzel, put this letter into the box, and hurry.   Ask for the newspaper at Mother Eberhardt's.   It's Saturday ; there must be news of the war."

I ran out, and put the letter in the village box. But the newspaper had not come.   Clémentz had been delayed by the snow, which did not surprise my uncle, as such things happened nearly every winter.

VIII

Returning from the post-office, I saw at a distance, in the large meadow behind the church Hans Aden, Frantz Sépel, and many of my other comrades, sliding on the pond. I could see a whole row of them give a sudden spring, and glide off like arrows, bending forward, their arms extended in the air to preserve their equilibrium, and I heard the prolonged whir of their wooden shoes on the ice, and their shouts of joy.

How my heart bounded as I watched them ! How I wished that I could join them ! Unfortunately Uncle Jacob was waiting for me, and I went in with my head full of this joyous sight. All the time we were at dinner, the idea of running down to the meadow never left me for a second ; but I was very careful not to speak of it to my uncle, for he always forbade my sliding on the pond for fear of accidents.

At last he went out to visit the curé, who was suffering from rheumatism. I waited until he had reached the main street, and then whistled to Scipio, and ran like a hare to Holly Lane. The dog bounded after me, and it was not until we reached the little lane full of snow, that we stopped to take breath. I thought I should find my comrades on the pond, but they had gone to dinner. On turning the corner of the church, I only saw the great deserted slides. I therefore had to slide alone, and as it was cold, I had enough of it in half an hour. I was returning to the village, when Hans Aden, Frantz Sépel, and two or three others, with red cheeks, cotton caps drawn over their ears, and hands in their pockets, came out from the hedges covered with snow.

" Is it you, Fritzel? " said Hans. " Are you going away? "

" Yes. I've just been sliding, and Uncle Jacob doesn't want me to slide. I'd rather go home."

" I split my shoe on the ice this morning," said Frantz, " and my father has mended it. Look ! "

He took off his shoe and showed it to us. His father had put a band of iron across it, fastened by four great nails, with pointed heads.

This made us laugh, and Frantz cried :

" There ! that isn't very fine for sliding ! Listen : let us go in a sled up the Altenberg, and we'll come down like the wind."

The idea of going in a sled seemed to me so magnificent, that I already saw myself on one, rushing down the hill, and guiding it with my heels, crying, in a voice which reached the clouds, " *Himmels-farth! Himmelsfarth!* " I was enchanted with the idea.

" Yes," said Hans Aden, " but how are we to get a sled? "

" Leave that to me," replied Frantz Sépel, the most mischievous of us all. " Father had one last year, but it was all worm-eaten, and grandmother made fire-wood of it. But it's all the same. Come on."

We followed him, full of doubt and hope. As we went down the street, we stopped before every shed, and looked up with envious eyes at the sleds hanging from the beams.

" There's a beautiful sled ! " said one ; " it could hold us all, easily."

" Yes," answered another, " but it would be too heavy to drag up the hill ; it is made of green wood."

" Ah," said Hans Aden, " but we'd take it for all that, if Father Gitzig would lend it to us. But he's a miser. He keeps his sled for himself alone ; as if sleds could wear out ! "

" Come on ! " cried Frantz Sépel, who was in advance.   All the party started again.   From time to time they glanced at Scipio, who kept near me.

" You have a fine dog," said Hans, " he's a French dog.   They have wool like sheep, and let you shear them without saying a word."

Frantz declared that he had seen, the year before, at the fair at Kaiserslautern, a French dog who wore glasses, and counted on a drum up to a hundred. He guessed all sorts of things, and Grandmother Anne thought he must be a sorcerer.

Scipio stopped and looked at us during this speech.   I was very proud of him.   Little Karl, the weaver's son, said that if Scipio were a sorcerer, he could get a sled for us ; but it would be necessary to give him our souls in exchange, and not one of us wanted to give him his soul.

So we went from house to house, and the church clock was striking two, when M. Richter passed us on his sled, crying to his great lean horse, " Get up ! Charlotte, get up ! "   The poor beast strained every nerve.   M. Richter, contrary to his custom, seemed very merry.   As he passed the butcher Sépel's house, he cried, " Good news, Sépel, good news ! " He cracked his whip, and Hans said :

" M. Richter's a little fuddled.   He must have found, somewhere, some wine which didn't cost him anything."

We laughed loudly at this ; for all in the village
knew that M. Richter was a miser. We had reached
the end of the street where stood the house of Father
Adam Schmitt, an old soldier of Frederic II., who
received a little pension to buy bread, and tobacco,
and occasionally schnapps.   He had been in the
Seven Years' War, and in all the campaigns of Silesia and Pomerania.   He was very old now, and
since his sister Roesel's death, lived alone in the last
house of the village—a little thatched house, having
only one room below, one above, and the roof with
its two attic windows.   There was also a shed on one
side, a pig-sty behind, and a little garden in front,
surrounded by a quick-set hedge, which Father
Schmitt cultivated with care.

Uncle Jacob liked this old soldier ; sometimes,
when he saw him passing the house, he would tap
on the window-pane, and cry, " Come in, Adam ! "
He always came in, knowing that uncle had real
French cognac in a cupboard, and that he called him
in to offer him a little glass.

We stopped, then, before his house, and Frantz,
leaning on the hedge, said :

" Look at that sled !   I bet Father Schmitt will
lend it to us, if Fritzel goes in boldly, puts his hand
beside the old man's ear, and says, ' Father Adam,

will you lend us your sled?' Yes, I bet he'll lend it to us ; I'm sure of it—only we must be bold ! "

I became very red. I looked at the sled with one eye, and with the other at the little low window on a level with the ground. All my comrades stood at the corner of the house, pushing me forward by the shoulder, saying :

" Go in, he'll lend it to you ! "

" I dare not," said I, speaking very low.

" You haven't any courage," replied Hans Aden; " if I were in your place, I'd go in at once."

" Let me look in, a little, and see if he's in good humor."

Then I peeped in at the little window, and saw Father Schmitt sitting on a stool before the stone hearth, on which a few coals burned amid a heap of ashes. His back was turned toward me. I could see only his long figure and stooping shoulders, his little blue cloth jacket, too short to reach the coarse gray linen pantaloons, his white hair falling on his neck, the blue cotton cap, with a little tassel in front, the large red ears standing out from his head, and great wooden shoes resting on the stove hearth. He was smoking his clay pipe, the bowl of which I could see projecting a little beyond his sunburnt cheek. This is all I saw beside the broken flag-stones of the floor, and on the left, a sort of manger filled with straw.   These observations did not inspire me with much confidence, and I tried to escape ; but the others pushed me into the entry, saying, in low voices :

" Fritzel—Fritzel—he'll lend it to you, I'm sure ! "

" No."

" Yes."

" I don't want to."

But Hans Aden had opened the door, and I was already in the room with Scipio, the others behind me, with wide-open eyes, staring and listening. Oh, how I wished I could escape !   Unfortunately, Frantz Sépel, outside, held the door half closed. There was room only for his head, and Hans Aden's, who stood on tip-toe behind him.   Old Schmitt had turned round.

" Why, it's Fritzel ! " said he, rising.   " What's the matter? "

He opened the door, and all the party fled like a flock of sparrows.   I was left alone.   The old soldier looked at me much astonished.

" What do you want, Fritzel? " asked he, taking a coal from the hearth to re-light his pipe, which had gone out.   Then seeing Scipio, he contemplated

him gravely, blowing great puffs of smoke.   I had
recovered my confidence a little.

"Father Schmitt," said I, "the boys want me
to ask you for your sled, to ride down the Altenberg."

The old soldier, who was opposite the dog, winked
and smiled.   Instead of replying, he rubbed his ear,
raising his cap, and asked :

"Is that your dog, Fritzel?"

"Yes, Father Adam ; he belongs to the woman
who is at our house."

"Ah, good ! he must be a soldier's dog.   He
must know the drill."

Scipio was watching us, with nose upturned, and
Father Schmitt, taking his pipe from his mouth,
said :

"He's a dog of the regiment.   He looks like old
Michel, whom we had in Silesia."   Then raising
his pipe, he cried : "Shoulder arms ! " in a voice
so loud that it resounded through the whole house.
But what was my surprise to see Scipio sit on his
hind legs, his fore legs hanging down, and carrying
himself like a real soldier.

"Ha! ha ! ha ! " cried old Schmitt, "I was
sure of it ! "

My comrades had all come back.   Some were

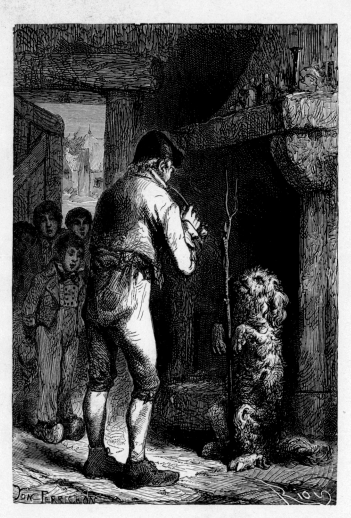

"CARRY ARMS!"

looking in through the half-open door, some through the window. Scipio did not stir, and Father Schmitt, as joyous as he had seemed grave before, said :

"Attention, march !" Then imitating the sound of a drum, he marched backward on his great wooden shoes, and began to cry, "March ! Pan— pan—rataplan. One—two. One—two !"

And Scipio marched with astonishing gravity, his long ears on his shoulders, and his tail curled. It was marvellous. My heart leaped. All the others were speechless with admiration.

"Halt !" cried Schmitt, and Scipio halted.

Then I thought no more of the sled ; I was so proud of Scipio's talents, that I would have run home and exclaimed to my uncle, "We have a dog who can drill !" But Hans Aden, Frantz Sépel, and all the rest, encouraged by the old soldier's good humor, had come in, and were standing there in ecstasy, their backs against the door, their caps under their arms.

"In place, rest !" cried Father Schmitt, and Scipio came down on his four paws, shaking his head, and scratching his neck with his hind leg, as if to say, "A flea has been biting me for two minutes, but one dares not scratch himself while under arms !"

I was speechless with joy at seeing these per-
formances, and dared not call Scipio for fear of making him ashamed.   But he placed himself near me,
modestly, which overwhelmed me with satisfaction.
I considered myself in some sort, a field-marshal at
the head of his armies.   All the others envied me.

Father Schmitt looked at Scipio with emotion.
We could see that he was recalling his soldier life.

" Yes," said he, in a few minutes, " he's a true
soldier's dog. But let us see if he understands politics, for very few dogs understand politics."   He
took a stick from behind the door, and held it cross-
wise, crying, " Attention to the word of command ! " Scipio was already in readiness.

" Jump for the Republic ! " cried the old soldier,
and Scipio leaped over the stick like a stag.

" Jump for General Hoche ! "   Scipio jumped.

" Jump for the King of Prussia ! "   But then he
seated himself on his tail very firmly, and the old
man began to laugh quietly, his eyes half shut, saying,

" Yes, he understands politics—ha ! ha ! ha !
Come ! "   He passed his hand over the dog's head,
and Scipio seemed very happy.

" Fritzel, you have a dog worth his weight in
gold ; he's a true soldier's dog."   And looking at

all of us, he added, " I'm going to lend you my sled, since you have such a good dog ; but you must bring it back at five o'clock, and take care not to break your necks."

He went out with us, and took his sled from the shed. My mind was divided between going to announce to my uncle Scipio's extraordinary talents, and riding down the Altenberg on our sled. But when I saw Hans Aden, Frantz Sépel, and all my companions, some before, some behind, pushing and pulling, galloping in ecstasy, I could not resist the pleasure of joining the party.

Schmitt watched us from the door :

" Take care not to upset," said he, again.

Then he went in, while we marched along in the snow. Scipio leaped at my side. I leave you to imagine our joy, our screams and shouts of laughter, as we went up the hill.

And when we were at the top, Hans Aden in front, his hands clinging to the sides of the sled, the rest behind, three together, Scipio in the middle, and the sled suddenly started, jolting in the ruts, and spinning over the slopes—what delight !

Ah ! we are never young but once.

The sled had hardly started, when Scipio sprang with one bound over our heads. He would rather

8

run, leap, bark, roll in the snow like a child, than go in a sled.   But this did not prevent us from retaining great respect for his talents.   Every time we went up, and he walked near us, full of dignity, first one, then the other would turn round, as we pushed our sled, and say :

" You're very fortunate, Fritzel, to have such a dog.   Adam Schmitt says he's worth his weight in gold."

" Yes, but he doesn't belong to them," cried another, " he's the woman's."

The idea that he was the woman's dog disturbed me very much, and I thought, " I hope they'll both stay at our house ! "

We continued to go up and down the hill until nearly four o'clock.   Then night began to fall, and we remembered our promise to Father Schmitt, and returned to the village.   As we drew near the old soldier's house we saw him standing at his door. He had heard us laughing and talking at a distance.

" Here you are," cried he ; " nobody's hurt?"

" No, Father Schmitt."

" So much the better."

He put his sled under the shed, and I ran off without saying " good-day," or " good-night," eager to announce to my uncle what a dog we had the

"AH! WE ARE ONLY YOUNG ONCE!"

honor of possessing. This idea made me so happy that I was home before I knew it. Scipio was at my heels.

"Uncle Jacob!" cried I, opening the door, "Scipio knows how to drill! Father Schmitt saw at once that he was a real soldier's dog. He made him march on his hind legs like a grenadier, only saying to him 'One! two!'"

My uncle was reading behind the stove. Seeing me so enthusiastic, he put his book on the mantelpiece, and said with an air of astonishment—

"Is it possible, Fritzel?"

"Yes," cried I, "and he understands politics, too: he leaps for the Republic and for General Hoche, but he won't leap for the King of Prussia."

My uncle laughed, and looked at the woman, who was also smiling, in the alcove, her elbow on the pillow.

"Madame Thérèse," said he, gravely, "you have not spoken of the remarkable talents of your dog. Is it true that Scipio knows so many fine things?"

"It is true, doctor," she said, caressing the dog, who had approached the bed, and stretched out his head to her, joyfully, "Yes, he knows all that,—he was the amusement of the regiment. Little Jean taught him something new every day. Isn't it so, my poor Scipio? Didn't you play at *drogue*,* shake the dice for good luck, and beat the reveille? How many times have our father and two elder brothers, when we halted for the night, been delighted to see you mount guard? You made everybody laugh by your air of gravity and your accomplishments ; we forgot the fatigue of the march as we gathered around you, and laughed heartily ! "

She said this in a tender voice, and was much moved, although smiling a little.

Scipio had straightened himself up, his paws on the edge of the bed, to listen to this praise.

But Uncle Jacob, seeing that Madame Thérèse became more and more agitated by these remembrances, feared they would do her harm, and said—

" I'm very glad, Fritzel, that Scipio knows how to drill, and understands politics ; but what have you been doing since noon ? "

" We've been on a sled up the Altenberg, Father Adam lent us his sled."

" That's very well, but all these doings have made us forget M. de Buffon and Klopstock. If this continues, Scipio will soon know more than you."

He rose and took from the bureau Buffon's Nat-

_____

* Game played by soldiers and sailors.

ural History, and put the candle on the table.
"Come, Fritzel," said he, smiling at my long face,
for I was wishing I had not returned so soon,
"Come!"

He sat down and took me on his knee. It seemed
very hard to return to M. de Buffon after eight days'
holiday; but my uncle had so much patience that I
was forced to have some also, and we began our
French lesson. It lasted an hour, until Lisbeth
came to lay the cloth. Then we turned round, and
saw that Madame Thérèse was dozing. My uncle
closed the book and drew the curtains, while Lisbeth
arranged the dishes.

IX

THAT evening, after supper, Uncle Jacob smoked his pipe in silence behind the stove. I sat before it, drying my pantaloons, Scipio's head between my knees, and watched the red firelight dancing on the floor. Lisbeth had taken away the candle as usual ; we were in darkness ; the fire burned briskly, as it does in very cold weather, the clock ticked slowly, and we could hear the old servant in the kitchen washing her dishes in the sink.

How many thoughts passed through my head, then ! Sometimes I thought of the dead soldier in Réebock's barn, and the black cock in the window. Sometimes of Father Schmitt making Scipio go through the drill ; then of the Altenberg and our descent on the sled. It all came back to me like a dream ; the plaintive murmur of the fire seemed to me the music of these remembrances, and I felt my eyes close softly.

About half an hour afterward I was awakened by

the sound of steps in the alley ; the door opened, and the mole-catcher's cheerful voice said :

" Snow, doctor, snow !   It's begun to fall again. We shall have it all night."

Uncle must have been dozing, for a minute passed before I heard him move, and answer :

" What would you have, mole-catcher?   This is the season.   We must expect it now."

Then he rose and went into the kitchen for a light.

The mole-catcher drew near.

" How, Fritzel here ! " said he. " You not asleep yet? "

My uncle returned.   I turned my head and saw that the mole-catcher had his winter clothes on ; his old cap of martin's fur,—the worn-out tail hanging down his back ; his goat-skin jacket,—the hair inside,—his red waistcoat with pockets hanging loosely on his hips, and old brown velvet breeches, adorned with patches on the knees.   He was smiling, half-shutting his small eyes, and holding something under his arm.

" Have you come for the Gazette, mole-catcher?" asked Uncle Jacob.   " It didn't come this morning. The messenger is behindhand."

" No, doctor, no.   I've come for something else."

He placed on the table an old square book, with a wooden cover at least a quarter of an inch thick, and covered with large brass ornaments, representing vine leaves. The edges were all blackened and greasy with age, and from each page hung strings and threads to mark the right places.

" See why I've come ! " said the mole-catcher, " I don't need news ; when I want to know what's going on in the world, I open, and look."

Then he smiled and his long yellow teeth showed themselves under the four hairs of his mustache, slender as needles.

My uncle said nothing, but drew the table near the stove, and sat down in his corner.

" Yes," continued the mole-catcher, " everything's in that, but one must understand—one must understand ! " touching his head dreamily. " The letters are nothing, it's the spirit—the spirit that one must understand."

Then he seated himself in the arm-chair, and took the book in his lap, with a sort of veneration ; he opened it, and said, while my uncle looked at him :

" Doctor, I've told you a hundred times about the book of my Aunt Roesel of Héming ; well, to-day I have brought it, to show you the past, the present, and the future. You will see! You will see!

All that has happened during the last four years, was written beforehand. I knew it well, but I wouldn't tell it because of that Richter, who would have laughed at me, for he can't see farther than the end of his nose. And the future, also, is here ; but I will only explain it to you, doctor, who are a sensible, reasonable, clear-sighted man. This is why I have come."

" Listen, mole-catcher," replied Uncle Jacob. " I know very well that all is mystery in this lower world, and I am not conceited enough to refuse to believe in predictions and miracles related by such wise authors as Moses, Herodotus, Thucydides, Livy, and many others. But nevertheless, I respect the will of God too much to wish to penetrate the secrets hidden by His infinite wisdom. I would rather see in your book the accomplishment of things already past, than the future. That will be clearer, too."

" Well, well, you shall know everything ! " said the mole-catcher, satisfied with my uncle's grave manner. He pulled his chair toward the table, and leaned the book on the edge, then rummaging in his pocket, drew out a pair of old brass spectacles, and put them on his nose, which gave him a very fantastic appearance. My interest may be imagined.

I too had approached the table, and leaning my elbows upon it, my chin in my hands, I watched him, holding my breath, my eyes staring from my head.

This scene will always be present to me ; the perfect silence of the room, the ticking of the clock, the murmur of the fire, the candle like a star in the midst of us ; opposite me my uncle in his dark corner, Scipio at my feet ; then the mole-catcher bending over his book of predictions, and behind him the little black window-panes, where the snow was falling in the darkness ; I see it all again, and it even seems as if I can hear the voice of the poor old mole-catcher, and that of good Uncle Jacob, both of whom have been so long in their graves.   It was a strange scene.

" How, mole-catcher," said my uncle, " you need glasses at your age?   I thought your sight was excellent."

" I don't need them to read ordinary things, nor to see out-of-doors ; I have good eyes.   From here I can see, in the spring, a nest of caterpillars in the trees on the side of the Altenberg.   But these glasses belonged to my Aunt Roesel of Héming, and it's necessary to have them on to understand this book.   Sometimes they trouble me, but I read over them or under them.   The principal thing is to have them on my nose."

" Ah, that's different, very different ! " said my uncle, seriously, for he was too kind-hearted to let the mole-catcher see that he was astonished.

The mole-catcher began to read : " ' A. D. 1793. —The grass is dry, the flower has fallen, because the wind has blown upon it.'   That means that it is winter ; the grass is dry, the flower has fallen because the wind has blown upon it."

My uncle nodded, and he continued ·:

" ' The isles saw, and were seized with fear, the ends of the earth were afraid ; they approached, and entered.'   That, doctor, means that England and even the farthest isles of the sea have become alarmed because of the Republicans.   ' They approached and entered.'   Everybody knows that the English have landed in Belgium to fight the French. But listen carefully to the rest.   ' In that time the leaders of the people will be like a fire in the midst of woods, and like a torch in the midst of sheaves. They will ravage the country right and left.' "

The mole-catcher then raised his finger gravely, and said :

" These are the kings and emperors who advance in the midst of their armies, and destroy everything in the countries which they cross.   Unhappily, we know these things from having seen them.   Our poor village will remember them a long time."

And as Uncle Jacob did not answer, he continued :

" ' In that time, woe to the unfaithful shepherd who shall abandon his flock ; the sword will fall from his hand, and his right eye will be entirely darkened.'   We see in these words the Bishop of Mayence, with his nurse and five mistresses, who made his escape last year on the arrival of General Custine.   He was truly an unfaithful shepherd, who caused scandal throughout the country ; his arm is withered, and his right eye is darkened."

" But," said my uncle, " remember, mole-catcher, that this bishop was not the only one, there were many more who behaved in the same manner, in Germany, France, Italy, and everywhere."

" The more reason, doctor ; the book speaks for all the world ; ' for,' said he, placing his finger on the page, ' for, in that time, said the Eternal, I will take away from the world, false prophets, doers of miracles, and the spirit of impurity.'   What can that mean, Dr. Jacob, but all these men who talk incessantly of loving our neighbors, to obtain our money ; who believe nothing, and menace us with hell ; who dress in purple and gold, and preach humility to us ; who say, ' Sell all your goods, and follow Christ,' and heap up riches upon riches in their palaces and convents ; who recommend faith to us, and laugh among themselves at the fools who listen to them? Isn't that the spirit of impurity? "

" Yes," said Uncle Jacob, " it is abominable."

" Well, it is for them, for all the bad shepherds, that these things are written."

Then he continued :

" ' In that time, there will be on the mountains, the noise of a multitude—of a great people who are rising—the noise of an assembled nation. The peoples round about will hear, and every man's heart will soften. And the haughty will be frightened. The world will be in travail ; the good will look at each other with burning faces ; they will hear for the first time great things spoken of ; they will know that all are equal in the sight of the Lord, that all have a right to justice, as the trees of the forest have to light ! ' "

" Is that written so, mole-catcher? " asked my uncle.

" You can see for yourself," answered the mole-catcher, handing him the book.

Uncle Jacob looked at it with a troubled expression.

" Yes, it is written," said he, in a low voice ; " it is written. Ah, may the Lord accomplish such great things in our time! May He rejoice our hearts with such a spectacle ! "

Then stopping suddenly, as if astonished at his own enthusiasm—

" Is it possible that at my age I allow myself to be so excited on this subject? I am a child, a real child ! "

He returned the book to the mole-catcher, who said, smiling,

" I see very well, doctor, that you understand this passage as I do ;—this noise of a great people rising, —it is France that proclaims the rights of man."

" How ! you believe that relates to the French Revolution? " asked my uncle.

" To what, then? 'tis as clear as the day."

Then he put on his glasses, which he had taken off, and read :

" ' There are seventy weeks in which to consummate the sin, to expiate the iniquity, to bring about the justice of ages. After which men will throw their idols of silver to the moles and bats. And the peoples will say, Let us beat our swords into ploughshares, and our spears into pruning hooks.' "

At this point the mole-catcher leaned his elbows

on the book, and rubbing his beard, with nose upturned, seemed to reflect profoundly. I could not
take my eyes from him. He seemed to me to see
strange things—an unknown world in the darkness
around us. The faint crackling of the fire and the
sighs of Scipio sleeping near me, produced on me the
effects of far-off human voices, and even the silence
disquieted me.

Uncle Jacob seemed to have recovered his calmness. He had just filled his large pipe, and lit it
with a piece of paper, slowly drawing two or three
puffs. He shut the lid and threw himself back in
his chair, with a sigh.

" ' Men will cast down their silver idols,' " said
the mole-catcher. "That is to say their crowns,
florins, and money of all kinds. ' They will throw
them to the moles.' That is to the blind, for you
know, doctor, that moles are blind. The unfortunate blind creatures, like Father Harich, are truly
moles. In broad daylight they walk in darkness,
as if under ground. In that time men will give
their money to the blind and to the bats. By bats
you must understand the old—old women, who are
no longer able to work, who are bald, and sit in their
chimney-corners, like Christine Besme, whom you
know as well as I. Poor Christine is so thin, and

has so little hair, that one naturally thinks when one sees her, ' she's a bat.' "

" Yes, yes," said my uncle, in a peculiar tone, nodding his head slowly, " it is clear, very clear. Now I understand your book ; it is something admirable."

" Men will give their money to the blind, and the old women, in the spirit of charity," continued the mole-catcher, " and that will be the end of misery in this world ; there will be no more poor people, ' in seventy weeks,' which are not weeks of days, but weeks of months. ' They will beat their swords into ploughshares, to cultivate the earth, and live in peace ! ' "

This explanation of the moles and bats had struck me so forcibly that I remained with eyes stretched wide open, imagining that I saw this wonderful transformation in the dark corner where my uncle sat. I had stopped listening, and the mole-catcher was continuing his monotonous reading, when the door opened again. I felt my flesh creep. If old Harich the blind man, and old Christine, had come in arm in arm, in their new forms, I would not have been more frightened. I turned with my mouth open,—and breathed freely ; it was our friend Koffel, who had come in. I had to look twice before I recognized him, my mind was so filled with thoughts of moles and bats.

Koffel wore his old gray winter jacket, a cloth cap drawn over his ears, and great shoes run down at the heels, in which he had put old slippers to go out in. He stood with knees bent and hands in his pockets, as if he were chilly ; innumerable flakes of snow covered him.

"Good-morning, doctor," said he, shaking his cap in the entry, "I am late ; so many people stopped me on the way to the 'Red Ox,' and the 'Little Gold Pitcher.'"

"Come in, Koffel. Did you close the alley gate?"

"Yes, Dr. Jacob, never fear."

He came in, and asked smilingly :

"The Gazette didn't come, this morning?"

"No, but we haven't needed it," said my uncle in a tone of comical good humor. "We have the mole-catcher's book, which relates the past, the present, and the future."

"Does it also relate our victory?" asked Koffel, approaching the stove. My uncle and the mole-catcher looked at each other in astonishment.

"What victory?" asked the latter.

"Ah, that of the day before yesterday, at Kaisers-

9

lautern. They are talking of nothing else in the village. It was Richter, M. Richter, who came up at two o'clock to bring the news. They've already emptied fifty bottles at the ' Little Gold Pitcher ' in honor of the Prussians; the Republicans are entirely put to rout! "

When he spoke of the Republicans we looked toward the alcove, fearing that the French woman might hear us. It pained us, for we knew that she was a good woman, and we thought this news would cause her much suffering. Uncle Jacob raised his hand and shook his head sadly, then got up softly and half-opened the curtains to see if Madame Thérèse was asleep.

" It is you, doctor," she said immediately; " I have listened to the mole-catcher's predictions for an hour; I have heard all."

" Ah, Madame Thérèse," said my uncle, " the news is false."

" I don't think so, doctor. From the moment a battle was fought at Kaiserslautern, day before yesterday, we must have been defeated; otherwise the French would have marched at once upon Landau to raise the siege, and cut off the retreat of the Austrians. Their right wing would have passed through the village." Then raising her voice,

" M. Koffel, will you tell me the details that you know."

This scene will always remain in my memory above all others, for we saw that night what a woman we had saved, and we learned, also, what that French race was which had risen *en masse* to convert the world.

The mole-catcher had taken the candle from the table and we were all in the alcove. I, at the foot of the bed, with Scipio beside me, looked on in silence, and saw for the first time that Madame Thérèse had become so thin that she looked like a man; her long bony face with its straight nose,— the shape of her eyes,—the sharp chin leaning on her hand; her lean brown arm was bared nearly to the elbow, escaping from the sleeves of Lisbeth's coarse chemise; a red silk handkerchief tied over her forehead hung down behind her neck. We could not see her beautiful black hair, but only some little locks over her ears, from which hung large gold rings. What particularly attracted my attention was a medal of bronze which hung from her neck, representing a young girl in a cap shaped like a casque. I knew afterward that it was the image of the Republic, but I thought it then the Holy Virgin of the French. As the mole-catcher raised the candle, the alcove was lighted up, and Madame Thérèse seemed to me much taller. Her feet, under the covering, reached the foot of the bed. I had never before noticed these things which impressed me then. She looked at Koffel, who looked anxiously at Uncle Jacob, as if to ask him what he must do.

"These are reports which are current in the village," said he with embarrassment; "that Richter is not to be relied upon."

"It is all the same, M. Koffel, tell me the news. The doctor allows it. Do you not, doctor?"

"Certainly," said my uncle, reluctantly, "but we must not believe all we hear."

"No—they exaggerate, I know very well; but it is better to know the truth than to imagine a thousand things; it is less tormenting."

Koffel then told us that two days before, the French had attacked Kaiserslautern, and from seven in the morning until night, had fought terribly, trying to enter the intrenchments; the Prussians had destroyed them by thousands; one saw only dead bodies in the ditches on the hill-sides, along the roads and in the Lauter. The French had abandoned everything; their cannon, army-wagons, guns and pouches. They were massacred everywhere, and Brunswick's cavalry, sent in pursuit, had taken a great number of prisoners.

Madame Thérèse, her chin leaning on her hand, her eyes fixed on the opposite wall, and lips compressed, said nothing. She listened, and when Koffel wished to stop, for it gave him much pain to relate these things before the poor woman,—she looked at him very calmly, and he continued, saying,

"They say this, or that, but I don't believe it."

At last he finished, and Madame Thérèse remained silent, lost in thought, for a few minutes. Then my uncle said:

"All these are only rumors;—we know nothing positively. You would do wrong to grieve, Madame Thérèse."

She raised herself slightly, leaning against the bedstead, and said very simply,

"Listen, it is clear that we have been repulsed. But do not think, doctor, that that discourages me. No; this affair, which seems very considerable to you, is but a little thing to me. I saw this same Brunswick arrive in Champagne, at the head of a hundred thousand veterans, uttering proclamations in which there was no common-sense, menacing all France, and then driven back by peasants in wooden shoes, at the point of the bayonet, as far as Prussia. My father,—a poor school-master, who had become major,—my brothers—poor laborers, who had become captains through their courage,— and I behind, with little Jean in my cart, escorted him, after the defiles of the Argonne and the battle of Valmy. Do not think then that these things alarm me. We are not a hundred thousand men, nor two hundred thousand; we are six million peasants, who mean to eat, ourselves, the bread that we have earned by our hard labor. It is just, and God is with us."

She said this with animation, extending her long bony arm. The mole-catcher, my uncle and Koffel looked at each other in stupefied amazement.

" It is not one defeat, nor twenty, nor a hundred which can conquer us," she continued. " When one of us falls, ten others rise. It is not for the King of Prussia, nor the Emperor of Germany, that we march; it is for the abolition of privileges of all kinds, for liberty, for justice, for the rights of man. In order to conquer us it will be necessary to ex- terminate every one of us," added she with a strange smile, " and that is not so easy as they may think. Only it is very unfortunate that so many thousands of good men, on your side, should suffer themselves to be massacred for kings and nobles, who are their greatest enemies, when simple good sense ought to tell them to join us, to drive away all these oppressors of the poor. Yes, this is very unfortunate, and gives me more pain than all the rest."

She lay down again, and Uncle Jacob remained silent for some moments, astonished at the justice of her words. The mole-catcher and Koffel looked at each other in silence; but it was easy to see that the Frenchwoman's reflections had struck them and that they were thinking:

" She is right! "

At last my uncle said:

" Be calm, Madame Thérèse, be calm! All will be well. We agree in many things; if it depended upon me, we would soon be at peace."

" Yes, doctor, I know it, for you are a just man, and we only want justice."

" Try to forget all that," said Uncle Jacob again. " Nothing is so necessary as quiet, if you wish to get well."

" I will try, doctor."

Then we came out of the alcove, and my uncle looking at us dreamily, said:

" It is almost ten o'clock. We must go to bed —it is time."

He saw Koffel and the mole-catcher out, and

pushed the bolt as usual. I had already gone up-stairs. That night I heard him walking in his room a long time. He paced up and down with the slow measured step of a man who is reflect-ing. At last every sound ceased, and I went to sleep under God's protection.

X

The next morning, when I awoke, my little windows were covered with snow. It will still falling so that I could not see the opposite house. Out-of-doors the bells of Uncle Jacob's sleigh were tinkling, and his horse, Rappel, was neighing, but no other sound was heard; the people in the village had all been careful to close their doors. I thought it must be something extraordinary that could call my uncle out in such weather, and after dressing, hurried downstairs to find out what it could be. The door was open; Uncle Jacob, up to his knees in snow, his large otter-skin cap drawn over his ears, and the collar of his overcoat turned up, was hastily arranging a bundle of straw in the sled.

" Are you going away, uncle? " I said, going to the door.

" Yes, Fritzel, yes, I'm going away," said he in a joyful tone. " Do you want to go with me? "

I liked very much to go in the sleigh, but seeing

137

the great snow-flakes whirling through the air, and thinking it would be cold, I answered:

" Another day, uncle; I'd rather stay at home to-day."

Then he laughed, and came in again, pinching my ear, as he always did when in a good humor. We went into the kitchen where the fire was dancing on the hearth, and giving out good heat. Lisbeth was washing dishes before the little window with round panes, which opened on the yard. All was quiet in the kitchen. The great soup tureens seemed to shine more than usual, and on their rounded sides danced fifty little flames, like those on the hearth.

" Now I'm ready," said my uncle, opening the larder, and putting a crust of bread in his pocket.

He put under his coat the flask of *kirschenwasser*, which he always carried in travelling. Then, as he was about to enter the sitting-room, his hand on the latch, he told the old servant not to forget his directions; to keep up good fires everywhere; to leave the door open that she might hear Madame Thérèse, and to give her all she asked for, except anything to eat,—for she must have only broth morning and evening, with vegetables,—and not to contradict her in anything. Then he went in, and I followed, thinking what pleasure I should have when he was gone, running about the village with my friend Scipio, and proudly displaying his talents.

"Well, Madame Thérèse," said Uncle Jacob, gayly, "here I am, ready for departure. What fine weather to go sleighing!"

Madame Thérèse raised herself on her elbow in the alcove—the curtains were drawn aside—and looked toward the windows with a melancholy expression.

"Are you going to see a patient, doctor?" said she.

"Yes, a poor wood-cutter of Dannboch, three leagues from here, who was run over by his sled. It is a serious injury and will allow of no delay."

"What a hard business yours is!" said she, sympathizingly. "To go out in such weather as this to help an unfortunate man, who will, perhaps, never appreciate your services."

"Ah, no doubt," said my uncle, filling his large porcelain pipe, "that has often happened, but what would you have? Because a man is poor is no reason why we should let him die; we are all brothers, Madame Thérèse, and the poor have a right to live as well as the rich."

"Yes, you are right, and yet how many in your place would remain quietly by their fireside, instead of risking their lives only for the pleasure of doing good." And raising her eyes expressively, she added: "Doctor, you are a Republican."

"I, Madame Thérèse! What do you mean?" cried he, laughing.

"Yes, a true Republican—a man who stops at nothing, who disregards all suffering, all privation, to do his duty."

"Well, if you understand it so, I am happy to deserve that name. But in all parties and all countries in the world, there are such men."

"Then, M. Jacob, they are Republicans without knowing it."

My uncle could not help smiling.

"You have a reply for everything," said he, putting his package of tobacco into the large pocket of his overcoat; "one cannot argue with you."

A few minutes' silence followed these words. My uncle struck a light. I had Scipio's head in my arms, and was thinking: "I hold you. You'll follow me. We'll come back to dinner, and then we'll go out again." The horse was neighing outside; Madame Thérèse was watching the great flakes

which fell against the panes, when my uncle, who
had lighted his pipe, said:

" I shall be absent until evening. But Fritzel
will keep you company. The time will not seem
too long."

He passed his hand through my hair, and I became as red as a lobster, which made Madame
Thérèse smile.

" Oh, no, doctor," said she, kindly, " it never
wearies me to be alone; we must let Fritzel run out
with Scipio; it will do them good. And they
would rather breathe the fresh air than be shut up
in the room—isn't it so, Fritzel? "

" Oh yes, Madame Thérèse! " replied I, giving
a great sigh of relief.

" How! aren't you ashamed to speak in that manner? " cried my uncle.

" Why not, doctor? Fritzel is like little Jean;
he says whatever he thinks, and he is right. Go,
Fritzel, run, amuse yourself: your uncle gives you
leave."

How I loved her then, and how sweet her smile
appeared to me! Uncle Jacob laughed, took his
whip from the corner behind the door, and said:

" Well, Madame Thérèse, *au revoir* and good
courage! "

"*Au revoir*, doctor," said she, with feeling, extending her slim hand to him. "Go, and heaven guard you."

They remained thus for some moments, thoughtful, then my uncle said:

"I shall be back this evening between six and seven, Madame Thérèse; have faith, be tranquil, and all will go well."

Then he went out. He sprang into the sleigh, wrapped his overcoat around his knees, touched Rappel with his whip, saying to me,

"Behave yourself, Fritzel!"

The sleigh glided noiselessly away up the street. Some good people who were looking from their windows, said:

"Dr. Jacob is surely called somewhere to a person dangerously ill, otherwise he would not travel in such a snow."

When my uncle had disappeared round the corner of the street, I closed the door, and went in to eat my soup by the fire. Scipio watched me, his great moustaches upturned, licking his mouth and winking. I let him have my plate to clean, as usual, which he did gravely, not greedily, like the other dogs in the village. We had finished, and were going out, when Lisbeth, who had just done her work, and was wiping her arms on the towel behind the door, said:

"What, Fritzel, are you not going to stay at home?"

"No, I'm going to see little Hans Aden."

"Well, listen. Since you've put on your boots, go to the mole-catcher's to get some honey for the Frenchwoman. The doctor wants her to have a drink with honey in it. Take your cup and go down there. Tell the mole-catcher it's for Uncle Jacob. Here's the money."

Nothing pleased me more than to have errands to do, especially at the mole-catcher's, who treated me as a reasonable man should. I took the cup, and started with Scipio for his house in Orties Lane, behind the church. Some gossips were beginning to sweep their sidewalks. At the inn of the Little Golden Pitcher we could hear the glasses and bottles tinkling. They were singing and laughing and going up and down stairs; which seemed to me extraordinary on Friday. I stopped to see if it were a wedding or a christening, and as I stood on tiptoe, on the other side of the street, looking into the little open entry, I saw, in the kitchen, the mole-catcher's singular profile bending over the fire, his black stump of a pipe in the corner of his mouth, his brown hand placing a coal on the tobacco. Farther on to the right I saw, too, old Grédel in her cap with floating ribbons. She was arranging plates on a dresser, and her gray cat walked on the edge of it, setting up her back, and holding her tail in the air.

In a moment the mole-catcher came slowly into the dark entry smoking his pipe. Then I cried:

" Mole-catcher! mole-catcher! "

He came to the edge of the steps, and said, laughing:

" Is it you, Fritzel? "

" Yes, I'm going to your house to get some honey."

" Well, come up, then, and take a drink. We'll go together at once." And turning toward the kitchen, " Grédel," cried he, " bring a glass for Fritzel."

I ran up the steps, and we went in, with Scipio at our heels. In the saloon we could see through the gray smoke, along the tables, men in blouses, in jackets, in waistcoats, their caps or felt hats drawn over their ears. Some seated in a row, others astride benches, raising their full glasses joyfully, and celebrating the great victory of Kaiserslautern. On all sides we heard them singing the

" *Fatherland.*" Some old women were drinking with their sons, and seemed as merry as the others.

I followed the mole-catcher toward the windows that overlooked the street. There we found friena Koffel and old Adam Schmitt in the corner, before a bottle of white wine. In the opposite corner were the innkeeper, Joseph Spick, his woollen cap drawn over his ears, like a bully, and M. Richter in hunting-jacket and great leather gaiters, drinking a bottle of green-sealed *gleiszeller*. They were both purple, up to their ears, and were shouting:

" To the health of Brunswick! To the health of our glorious army! "

" Here! " said the mole-catcher, approaching our table, " make room for a man! "

And Koffel, turning round, shook my hand while Father Schmitt said:

" Well and good, well and good, here's a re-inforcement for us! "

He seated me near him, against the wall, and Scipio came immediately to rub his hand with the end of his nose, with the air of an old acquaintance.

" Ha! ha! ha! " said the old soldier: " it's you, old fellow—you know me! "

Grédel brought a glass, and the mole-catcher
10

filled it. At that moment, M. Richter cried sneeringly, from the other end of the table:

"Ha, Fritzel! how's Dr. Jacob? He doesn't come to celebrate the great battle! It is astonishing, astonishing, such a good patriot!"

And I, not knowing what to reply, said in a low tone to Koffel:

"Uncle has gone in his sleigh to see a poor wood-cutter, who was run over by his sled."

Then Koffel, turning, cried in a clear voice—

"While the grandson of Salm-Salm's old servant stretches out his legs under the table, near the stove, and drinks *gleiszeller* in honor of the Prussians who laugh at him, Dr. Jacob goes through the snow to see a poor wood-cutter on the mountain, who has been run over by his sled. That pays less than lending money on heavy interest, but it shows more heart, nevertheless."

Koffel had drunk a little too much, and all the men were listening and smiling. Richter, with a long face and compressed lips, did not answer at first, but after a moment he said—

"What wouldn't we do for the love of the Rights of Man, for the Goddess of Reason, and the Maximum, above all when a real *citoyenne* encourages you!"

" M. Richter, be silent! " cried the mole-catcher in a loud voice. " Dr. Jacob is as good a German as you, and that woman, of whom you speak without knowing her, is a good woman. Dr. Jacob has only done his duty in saving her life. You ought to be ashamed to excite the men of the village against a poor sick creature who can't defend herself: it's abominable! "

" I'll be silent when it suits me," cried Richter in his turn. " You talk very loud—one would think that the French had gained the victory! "

Then the mole-catcher, his face as red as fire, struck his fist on the table, making the glasses fall over. He partly rose, but reseated himself, and said:

" I have a right to rejoice in the victories of old Germany, at least quite as much as you, M. Richter, for I am a old German like my father, and my grandfather, and all the mole-catchers known for two hundred years in the village of Anstatt for the raising of bees, and the catching of moles; while the cooks of the Salm-Salms wandered through France with their masters, to turn the spit, and lick the bottom of the pots."

Everybody in the room burst out laughing at this speech, and M. Richter, seeing that most of them were against him, judged it prudent to be moderate, and replied, therefore, in a calm tone:

" I've never said anything against you nor Dr. Jacob; on the contrary, I know that the doctor's an able man, and an honest man. But that doesn't prevent every good German from rejoicing on such a day. For, listen, it's not an ordinary victory, it's the end of that famous Republic, ' one and indivisible.' "

" How! how! " cried old Schmitt, " the end of the Republic? That's a piece of news! "

" Yes, it won't last six months longer," said Richter with assurance, " for, from Kaiserslautern the French will be driven to Hornbach, from Hornbach to Sarrebruck, to Metz, and thus to Paris. Once in France we will find crowds of friends to help us; the nobility, the clergy, and the respectable people are all on our side. They only await the coming of our army to rise. And as to this troop of beggars, gathered from right and left, without officers and without discipline, what can they do against old soldiers, firm as rocks, advancing in order of battle, under the lead of the old warrior race? Crowds of bunglers without a single general, without even a real corporal *schlague!* Peasants, mendicants, true ' *sans culottes*,' as they call themselves,—I ask you what can they do against Brunswick, Wurmser, and hundreds of other old captains, tried by all the perils of the Seven Years' War? They will be scattered and will perish by thousands like grasshoppers in autumn."

Everybody in the room seemed to be of Richter's opinion, and several said:

"Well and good, he speaks truly. We've thought the same for a long time."

The mole-catcher and Koffel were silent; but old Adam Schmitt shook his head and smiled. After a moment's silence he laid his pipe on the table, and said:

"M. Richter, you speak like an almanac; you predict the future in an admirable manner; but it's not all so clear to others as to you. I am willing to believe that the old race is born to make generals, since nobles all come into the world captains. But occasionally generals can also come from the race of peasants, and they do not make the worst ones, for they become generals through their own bravery. These Republicans, who seem to you such fools, have sometimes good ideas, for all that; for example, they have a rule that any one can become a field-marshal, if he have the courage and capacity; on this account all the sol-

diers fight furiously. They hold in their ranks as
firmly as if they were nailed, and march forward
like cannon balls, for they know that if they dis-
tinguish themselves they have a chance of becoming captains, colonels, or generals. The Germans
fight to give themselves masters; the French fight
to get rid of them; which makes a great difference.
I watched them from Father Diemer's window, on
the first floor, opposite the fountain, during the two
charges of the Croats and lancers—magnificent
charges;—well, it astonished me very much, M.
Richter, to see how those Jacobins bore themselves.
And their colonel gave me real pleasure, with his
great Lorraine peasant's face, and small wild-boar's
eyes. He wasn't as well dressed as a Prussian
major, but he sat his horse as tranquilly as if they
were playing an air on the clarionet for him. They
retreated at last, it is true, but they had a division
at their backs, and left only the guns and pouches
of the dead on the square. Such soldiers, believe
me, M. Richter, are men of expedients. The old
warrior races are good, but the young grow in their
shade, as young oaks under large ones, and when
the old decay the young take their place. I do not
believe, therefore, that the Republicans run away
as you say. They are already famous soldiers, and

if a general or two comes, take care! And this is not at all impossible, for among twelve or fifteen hundred thousand peasants there's more choice than between ten or twelve thousand nobles. The race is not so fine, perhaps, but it's stronger!"

Old Schmitt stopped a moment to take breath, and then, as everybody was listening, added—

"Here am I, for example; if I had had the happiness of being born in such a country, do you believe that I would have contented myself with being Adam Schmitt, with a pension of a hundred florins, six wounds and fifteen campaigns? No, no, drive that idea out of your head. I should have been captain, colonel or general Schmitt, with a good pension of two thousand dollars, or else my bones would have been resting somewhere, long ago. When courage is a highway to distinction, one has courage, and when it serves only to make one a sergeant and promote the nobles, each one takes care of his skin."

"And education," cried Richter, "do you count education nothing? Is a man who don't know how to read worth as much as a Duke of Brunswick who knows everything?"

Then Koffel, turning, said calmly,

"You are right, M. Richter, education makes

half, perhaps three-quarters of a man. This is why these Republicans fight to the death; they wish their sons to receive education as well as the nobles. It is the want of education which causes bad conduct and poverty; poverty causes wicked temptations, and wicked temptations lead to all the vices. The greatest crime of those who govern in this world is refusing education to the poor, so that their noble race may always be above them. It is as if they put out people's eyes when they come into the world, to profit by their labor. God will avenge these sins, M. Richter, for He is just. And if the Republicans shed their blood, as they say, to prevent such abuses, all religious men who believe in immortality ought to approve of them." So Koffel spoke, adding that if his parents had been able to educate him, he might perhaps have done honor to Anstatt, and have been of some use, instead of being a poor devil.

Every one agreed with him, and several said among themselves:

"What would we have been if we had been educated? Are we more stupid than other people? No, heaven gives to all the bright sun and the heavy dew. We had good intentions: we appealed for justice; but they left us in the darkness, in a spirit of calculation, to keep us down. These men think to elevate themselves by preventing others from rising; it is abominable!"

And I, remembering how much trouble Uncle Jacob had taken to teach me to read in Buffon, repented that I had not profited more by his lessons, and was much affected. M. Richter, seeing everybody against him, and not knowing how to reply to Koffel's judicious words, shrugged his shoulders as if to say, "These are fools inflated with pride, creatures who need to be brought to reason." But silence was beginning to prevail, and the mole-catcher had just ordered a second bottle to be brought, when dull growls were heard under the table. We at once saw M. Richter's great red dog walking around Scipio. This dog was called Max; his hair was short, his nose flat, and his ribs protruding; he had yellow eyes, long ears, and tail raised like a sabre. He was large, lean and muscular. M. Richter was accustomed to hunt with him whole days without giving him anything to eat, under pretext that good hunting dogs ought to be hungry to scent the game and follow in its track. He wanted to get behind Scipio, who kept turning round, his head raised, and his lips trembling. Looking toward M. Richter, I saw that he was

slily urging his dog on. Father Schmitt noticed it
also, for he said:

"M. Richter, you are wrong to urge your dog.
This spaniel you see is a soldier's dog, full of cun-
ning, and knows all the stratagems of war. Yours
may be of an old race, but take care—this dog's
capable of strangling him."

"Strangle my dog!" cried Richter. "He could
swallow ten like this miserable cur. With a single bite he could break his back!"

When I heard this, I wanted to run away with
Scipio, for M. Richter was urging his great Max,
and all the drinkers turned round, laughing, to see
the battle. I was going to cry, but old Schmitt
held me by the shoulder, saying in a low voice:

"Be quiet, be quiet,—fear nothing, Fritzel. I
tell you our dog understands politics—the other
is only a great beast that has seen nothing of the
world." And turning to Scipio, he said to him
again and again, "Attention! attention!"

Scipio did not stir. He stood back in the corner of the window, his head erect, his eyes shining
under his thick curly hair, and in the corner of his
trembling moustache we could see one very sharp-
pointed white tooth. The big red dog advanced,
his head stretched forward, and his hair standing

up on his lean back. They both growled; then Max made a leap to seize Scipio by the throat. Three or four short, terrible cries were heard. Scipio had bent down while the other caught him by the hair, and with one bite he snapped at his paw. Then you should have heard Max's distressing cries, and seen him steal off, limping, under the tables; he fled like lightning between the legs of the guests, repeating his sharp cries, which pierced one's ears. M. Richter rose furiously to attack Scipio, but the mole-catcher took his stick from behind the door, and said:

"M. Richter, if your great beast is bitten, whose fault is it? You urged him on to do it. If he is maimed now, it will teach you better."

And old Schmitt, laughing and crying, called Scipio between his knees, and said,

"I knew very well that he understood the stratagems of war! He! he! he! we've brought off the flags and the cannon!"

All his audience laughed with him, so that M. Richter angrily kicked his dog into the street so as not to hear his cries. He would have been glad to do the same to Scipio, but everybody was astonished at the dog's courage, and natural good sense.

"Come," cried the mole-catcher, rising, "come

now, Fritzel, it's time I gave you what you wanted. I congratulate you, M. Richter; you have a famous dog. Grédel, set down two bottles on the slate."

Schmitt and Koffel also rose, and we all went out together, laughing heartily. Scipio kept near us, knowing that he had nothing good to hope for when we were gone. At the foot of the steps, Schmitt and Koffel turned to the right to go down the main street, and the mole-catcher and I crossed the square, on the left, to Orties Lane. The mole-catcher walked in front, stooping, one shoulder higher than the other, as was his habit, drawing great puffs, one after another, from his pipe, and laughing to himself, doubtless at the remembrance of Richter's discomfiture. We soon arrived at his small door, which was in the basement. As we went down the steps he said to me:

"Come, Fritzel, come; leave the dog outside, for there's none too much room in the hole."

He was right in calling his hut a "hole," for it had only two little windows, even with the ground, opening on the street. Inside, all was dark; the large bed and the wooden staircase, the old stools, the table covered with saws, brads and tweezers, the wardrobe adorned with two squashes, the ceiling

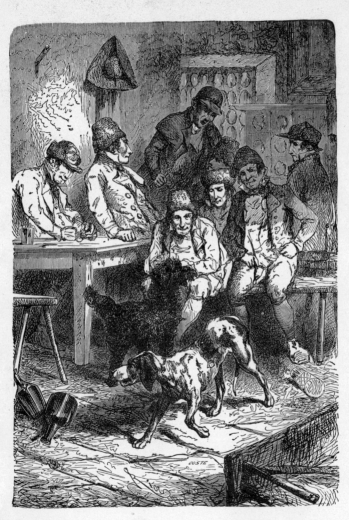

THEN YOU OUGHT TO HAVE HEARD THE PLAINTIVE CRIES OF MAX.

crossed by poles where old Berbel, the mole-catch-er's mother, hung the hemp which she had spun; traps of all sorts placed on the canopy of the bed, in an alcove gray with dust and cobwebs; hundreds of martens' and weasels' skins hanging from the walls, some turned inside out, others still fresh and stuffed with straw to dry them;—all these left you hardly room enough to turn round, and the thought of them recalls the happy time of my youth, for I have seen them a hundred times, summer and win-ter, rain or shine, whether the little windows were open or shut. I always picture the mole-catcher to myself, in that room, seated at the table, showing his traps, his mouth twisted, lips compressed, and old Berbel,—yellow-skinned, her horse-hair cap on the back of her head, her little dry hands with long black nails, streaked with large blue veins, spin-ning from morning till night beside the stove. Once in a while she would raise her old wrinkled face, and look at her son with an air of satisfaction. But that day Berbel was not in a good humor, for we had hardly entered before she began to scold the mole-catcher in a sharp voice, declaring that he was passing his life at the tavern, that he thought of nothing but drinking, and did not provide for the future—false charges, to which the mole-

catcher did not reply, knowing that he must hear all
his mother said without complaining. He quietly
opened the closet while old Berbel scolded, and
took from the highest shelf a large glazed earthen
pot, in which honey as yellow as gold, in combs
white as snow, lay in regular layers. He put it on
the table, and taking out two fine combs, which he
put on a very clean plate, said to me:

"Here's some beautiful honey for the French
lady, Fritzel. Honey in the comb is the best thing
in the world for sick people. It is nicer, and then
it is so fresh and wholesome!"

I had already placed the money on the edge of
the table, and Berbel was stretching out her hand
for it, very willingly, but the mole-catcher gave it
back to me.

"No," said he, "no; I won't be paid for it; put
the money in your pocket, Fritzel, and take the
plate. Leave your pot here. I'll take it to you this
evening, or to-morrow morning." And as the old
woman seemed angry, he added: "Tell the French
lady, Fritzel, that the mole-catcher makes her a
present of this honey with pleasure—do you hear?
—with all his heart—for she's a respectable woman. Don't forget to say 'respectable,'—do you
mind?"

" Yes, mole-catcher, I'll tell her. Good-day, Berbel," said I, opening the door.

She answered by nodding her head abruptly. The avaricious old woman would not say anything on Uncle Jacob's account, but it seemed very hard to her to see the honey going without being paid for. The mole-catcher saw me out, and I turned homeward, well satisfied with what had just happened.

XI

At the corner of the church I met little Hans
Aden, who was coming back from sliding on the
pond. He turned round, his hands in his pockets up to his elbows, and called out:

"Fritzel! Fritzel!"

When I came up, he looked at the honey, and
said:

"Is that for you?"

"No, it's to make a drink for the French lady."

"I'd like to be sick in her place," said he, licking
his thick lips, expressively. Then he added: "What
are you going to do this afternoon?"

"I don't know—I shall go to walk with Scipio."

He looked at the dog, and stroking his back, said:

"Listen: if you'd like, we'll go to lay traps
behind the dunghills of the Postthâl; there are
a good many greenfinches and sparrows along the
hedges, under the sheds, and in the trees of the
Postthâl."

" I'd like it very much," said I.

" Yes, meet me here on the steps. We'll go together."

Before we parted, Hans asked me to let him put his finger on the bottom of the plate. I assented, and he found the honey very good. After which, each of us took his own way, and I reached home about half-past eleven.

" Ah, here you are!" cried Lisbeth, as I entered the kitchen; " I thought you were never coming back. Heavens! must you take so much time to do an errand?"

I told her about my meeting the mole-catcher on the steps of the Little Golden Pitcher, the dispute of Koffel, old Schmitt and the mole-catcher with M. Richter, the great battle between Max and Scipio, and finally the manner in which the mole-catcher had told me to say that he wanted no money for his honey, and that he offered it with all his heart to the French lady, who was a " respectable " person. As the door was open, Madame Thérèse heard me, and told me to come in. I saw that she was touched, and when I gave her the honey she accepted it.

" Well, Fritzel, well," said she with tears in her eyes, " I am pleased, much pleased with this present.

11

The respect of honest men always gives us much pleasure. I will thank the mole-catcher myself, when he comes."

Then she leaned forward, and put her hand on the head of Scipio, who was standing beside the bed, looking up at her. She smiled, and said:

"Scipio, you also sustain the good cause, then?"

The dog, seeing joy sparkle in her eyes, began to bark loudly. He fell back on his hind legs, as if to go through the drill.

"Yes, yes, I'm better now," said she, "I feel much stronger. Ah! we have suffered so much!"

Then, sighing, she leaned back on the pillow, and said:

"Good news—only good news, and all will be well!"

Lisbeth had finished setting the table. She said nothing, and Madame Thérèse fell into a revery. The clock struck twelve, and a few minutes after the old servant brought in the little tureen of soup for herself and me. She made the sign of the cross, and we ate our dinner.

Every moment I turned my head to see if Hans Aden was already on the church steps. Madame Thérèse had lain down again, turning her back to us, and drawing the blanket over her. Doubtless

she had still much uneasiness. I thought only of the
dunghills of the Postthâl. Already I could see our
brick traps, placed around in the snow, the lids
raised, supported by two little wooden sticks, and
grains of wheat scattered on the edge and in the
bottom. I saw the greenfinches flying from tree to
tree, and the sparrows in a row on the edges of the
roofs, calling, watching, listening, while we, hidden
in the shed behind heaps of hay, waited, our hearts
throbbing with impatience. Then a sparrow would
light on the dunghill, his tail spread out like a fan—
then another, then all the flock. There they are!
There they are! near our traps! They're coming
down—three of them are hopping about and peck-
ing at the grains of wheat. *Frouu!* they all fly
away at once. It's some noise on the farm—it's the
boy Yéri with his great wooden shoes, who's just
shouted to one of the horses in the stable, " Come,
turn round, Foux! " What a misfortune! If the
horses were only dead, and Yéri with them! Well,
we must still wait—the sparrows have gone far
away. Suddenly one of them begins to cry again
—they are coming back to the roof. Ah! if Yéri
will only not shout again—if he'll only be quiet—
if there were only no people on the farm nor in
the road! What anxiety! At last one comes down

again—Hans pulls my jacket—we hold our breath—we are dumb with hope and fear! All this I saw beforehand that I could not keep quiet.

"In heaven's name, what's the matter with you?" said Lisbeth. "You're fidgeting like a soul in torment—do keep still."

I did not hear her, with my nose flattened against the window-pane: I was thinking—

"Will he come or won't he come? Perhaps he's already down there—he may have taken somebody else with him!"

This idea seemed terrible to me.

I was going to run out, when at last I saw Hans Aden crossing the Square. He was looking toward our house, watching for me. I was already in the alley, and opened the gate without calling Scipio this time. Then I ran close to the wall, for fear of some errand or other hindrance;—so many misfortunes do happen to one in this world! It was not till we were far from the house, in Orties Lane, that Hans and I stopped to take breath.

"Have you some wheat, Hans?"

"Yes."

"And your knife?"

"Be easy—here it is. But, Fritzel, I can't carry everything—you must take the bricks, and I'll take the tiles."

" Yes; come on."

And we crossed the fields back of the village,
through snow up to our waists.   If the mole-
catcher, Koffel, or my uncle, himself, had called
us then, we would have run on like thieves, without turning our heads.

We soon came to the old abandoned kiln, for they
rarely bake bricks in the winter, and took our load
of bricks.   Then, re-crossing the meadow, we
climbed over the hedges of the Postthâl, all covered
with frost, just opposite the large square dunghills
back of the stables and out-house.   We could see
the sparrows far above us, sitting in a row on the
edges of the roofs.

" I told you so," cried Hans; " listen—listen! "

Then we placed our traps, clearing away the snow
from the ground.   Hans cut little sticks, placed the
tiles very carefully, and then scattered wheat all
around.   The sparrows watched us from the roofs,
lightly turning their heads, without moving a wing.
Hans rose, wiping his nose on the back of his sleeve,
and looking up, winking, so as to see the sparrows.

" Come," said he in a low voice, " they're going
to come down."

We went into the shed, full of high hopes,—and
at that moment all the flock disappeared.   We

thought they would come back; but until nearly four o'clock we remained squatted down behind the heaps of hay, without hearing the cry of a single sparrow. They understood what we were doing, and had flown far away to the other end of the village.

Imagine our despair! Hans, notwithstanding his good disposition, was terribly angry, and I indulged in the saddest reflections, thinking there was nothing more foolish than wanting to catch sparrows in the winter, when they were nothing but skin and bones,—and it would take four of them to make a mouthful.

At last, tired of waiting, and seeing that it was getting dark, we returned to the village through the main street, shivering, with our hands in our pockets, moist noses, and caps drawn over our ears, in a dismal manner.

It was night when I got home. Lisbeth was preparing supper; but as I felt rather ashamed to tell her how the sparrows had fooled us, I opened the door of the sitting-room softly, and sat down quietly behind the stove, instead of running into the kitchen as usual.

Nothing stirred. Scipio was sleeping under the arm-chair curled up in a heap, and I had been warming myself for a quarter of an hour, listening to the murmur of the fire. When Madame Thérèse, whom I thought had been asleep, said in a gentle voice:

"Is that you, Fritzel?"

"Yes, Madame Thérèse," answered I.

"Are you warming yourself?"

"Yes; Madame Thérèse."

"You were very cold, then?"

"Oh, yes."

"What have you been doing this afternoon?"

"Hans Aden and I've been setting traps for the sparrows."

"Did you take many?"

"No, Madame Thérèse, not many."

"How many?"

It made my heart bleed to tell this kind woman that we had not taken any.

"Two or three, didn't you, Fritzel?" asked she.

"No, Madame Thérèse."

"Didn't you take any, then?"

"No."

She was silent, and I thought she must feel very sorry.

"They are very smart birds," she said in a moment.

"Oh, yes."

" Are your feet wet, Fritzel? "

" No, I had on my wooden shoes."

" Well, well, so much the better. Be comforted; another time you'll be more fortunate."

While we were talking Lisbeth came in, leaving the kitchen door open.

" Ah, here you are," said she; " I'd like to know where you spend your days? Always out, always with your Hans Aden or your Frantz Sépel."

" He's been catching sparrows," said Madame Thérèse.

" Sparrows! if I could only see them once," cried the old servant. " Every winter for three years, he has run after sparrows. Once he caught by chance in the autumn an old featherless jay, who had no strength left to fly, and since then he thinks all the birds of heaven are his."

Lisbeth laughed. She sat down to the spinning-wheel, and said, as she dipped her finger into the *mouilloir.**

" Now everything's ready, and when the doctor comes I'll only have to lay the cloth:—What was I telling you about a little while ago? "

" You were speaking of your conscripts, M'lle Lisbeth."

* Vessel of water, in which women wet their fingers when spinning flax.

" Ah, yes—when this wicked war began all the young men of the village went away—big Ludwig, the blacksmith's son, little Christel, Hans Gœrner, and many others—they went, some on foot, some on horseback, singing, '*Fatherland! Fatherland!*' with their comrades who took them to Kirschtâl, to Father Fritz's inn, on the road to Kaiserslautern. They sang, indeed, but that did not prevent them from crying bitterly when they saw the steeple of Anstatt for the last time. Little Christel embraced Ludwig at every step, saying, ' When shall we see Anstatt again?' Ludwig answered: ' Ah, alas! we mustn't think of that; the good God will protect us from these Republicans, heaven confound them!' They wept together, and the old sergeant, who had come expressly for them, kept saying, ' Forward! Courage! We are men!' His nose was red from drinking with our conscripts. Tall Hans Gœrner, who was going to marry Rosa Mutz—the *garde champêtre's* daughter—cried, ' One drink more! one drink more! This is perhaps the last plate of sour-krout that we shall ever see!' "

" Poor boy!" said Madame Thérèse.

" Yes," answered Lisbeth, " and yet that would be nothing if the girls could be married. But when the boys go away, the girls are left here, to dream from morning till night, to wear themselves out and die off. They can't marry the old men,—sixty years old,—widowers, or else hump-backed, lame, or one-eyed. Ah! Madame Thérèse, I don't reproach you; but without your Revolution we would have been very happy, we would only think of praising God for his goodness. Such a Republic, which throws everything into disorder, is terrible! "

As I listened to this speech I noticed that a pleasant odor of stuffed veal was filling the room, and Scipio and I at last got up to take a look in the kitchen. We found a good onion soup, a breast of veal, stuffed, and fried potatoes. Running about had made me so hungry that it seemed as if I could swallow the whole at a mouthful.

Scipio was no less favorably inclined; with his foot on the edge of the hearth he snuffed among the pots, for a dog's nose, as M. de Buffon says, is a very delicate second sight. After taking a good look, I prayed for my uncle's return.

" Ah, Lisbeth," cried I, re-entering the sitting-room, " if you knew how hungry I am! "

" So much the better," replied the old woman, who was still talking, " an appetite's a good thing."

Then she continued her village tattle, to which Madame Thérèse seemed to listen with pleasure. I went backwards and forwards, from the sitting-room to the kitchen, and Scipio followed me; doubtless he felt the same as I did. Outside, the night was growing dark. Occasionally Madame Thérèse would interrupt the old servant, raising her finger, and saying:

"Listen!"

Then we would all be quiet a moment.

"It's nothing," said Lisbeth; "Hans Bockel's cart is passing," or else, "it's mother Dreyfus, who is going to watch at the Brêmers'."

She knew the habits of everybody in Anstatt, and it gave her real happiness to talk to the French lady about them, now that she had seen the image of the Holy Virgin hanging from her neck;—for the sudden friendship sprang from that, as I learned afterward.

Seven o'clock struck,—then the half hour. At last, not knowing how to pass the time, while waiting, I climbed on a chair, and took from a shelf Buffon's Natural History,—a thing which I had never done before. Then, with my elbows on the table, in a kind of despair, I began to read French alone. Only a ravenous appetite could have given me such an idea; but every moment I raised my head and listened, looking toward the window with eyes wide open. I had just finished the account of the sparrow, which possesses twice as much brain as man in proportion to its size, when a sound was heard afar off, the sound of little bells. It was still a hardly perceptible tinkling, lost in the distance, but it approached rapidly, and soon Madame Thérèse said:

"It is the doctor."

"Yes," said Lisbeth, rising and putting her wheel in the corner by the clock; "this time it's he."

She ran into the kitchen. I was already in the passage, leaving Buffon on the table, and I opened the outer door, crying,

"Is it you, uncle?"

"Yes, Fritzel," replied my uncle's cheerful voice. "I have come. Is all well at home?"

"Very well, uncle, everybody's well."

"Good, good!"

Then Lisbeth went out with the lantern, and I saw Uncle Jacob in the shed unharnessing the horse. He was white, in the midst of the darkness, and every hair of his coat and fur cap shone like a star in the light of the lantern. He was in a hurry; Rappel, turning his head toward the stable, seemed as if he could not wait.

"Good Lord, how cold it is out here!" said the

old servant, running to help him. "You'll be frozen, doctor. Go in, quick, and warm yourself. I'll finish this by myself."

But Uncle Jacob was not accustomed to leave the care of his horse to others; and it was not till he saw Rappel before the rack filled with hay, with his feet in the good straw, that he said:

"Now we'll go in."

And we went in together.

"Good news, Madame Thérèse!" cried he in the doorway. "Good news! I've come from Kaiserslautern; it is all right down there."

Madame Thérèse, seated on her bed, looked at him very pale. And as he shook his cap, and took off his overcoat, she said:

"How, doctor, do you come from Kaiserslautern?"

"Yes, I went as far as that—I wanted to know all the particulars. I've seen everything—I've informed myself of everything," said he, smiling, "but I won't conceal from you, Madame Thérèse, that I'm dying of hunger and fatigue."

He was seated in the arm-chair, drawing off his heavy boots, and watching Lisbeth lay the cloth with eyes as sharp as Scipio's and mine.

"All I can tell you," said he, rising, "is that

the battle of Kaiserslautern is not so decisive as they thought, and your regiment was not engaged. Little Jean has run no new dangers."

"That is enough," said Madame Thérèse, lying back with an air of happiness and unspeakable emotion, "that is enough. You need tell me no more, lest I should be too happy. Warm yourself, doctor; eat—don't hurry. I can wait now."

Lisbeth brought in soup, and my uncle, sitting down, said again:

"Yes, that is positive. You can be easy on these two points. I'll tell you the rest presently."

Then we began to eat, and my uncle, looking at me now and then, smiled, as if to say:

"I believe you want to keep up with me. What in the devil has given you such an appetite?"

Our great hunger was soon appeased. We remembered poor Scipio, who was watching us stoically, and now it was his turn to eat. My uncle took another good drink, then lighted his pipe, and approaching the alcove took Madame Thérèse's hand, as if to feel her pulse, and said:

"Here I am!"

She smiled, and said nothing.

Then he drew up the arm-chair, opened the curtains, placed the candle on the night-table, and began the history of the battle. I listened, leaning on the back of his chair. Lisbeth remained standing in the sitting-room, in the dark.

"The Republicans arrived before Kaiserslautern on the evening of the 27th," said he; "the Prussians had been there for three days. They had fortified the position, by placing cannon on the heights that command the plateau. General Hoche followed them from the line of the Erbach; he had even wished to surround them at Bisingen, and he immediately resolved to attack them the next day. The Prussians had forty thousand men and the French thirty thousand. The next day the attack began on the left; the Republicans, under General Ambert, began to scale the heights, at a charge, crying, 'Landau or death!' At this moment, Hoche ought to have attacked the centre. But it was covered by woods and heights. It was impossible for him to arrive in time. General Ambert was obliged to retreat before the Prussian fire; he had all Brunswick's army against him. The day following, November 29th, Hoche attacked the centre; General Ambert was to turn the right wing, but he lost his way in the mountains, so that Hoche was overpowered in his turn. In spite of this the attack was to recommence the next day, November

30th. That day Brunswick made a movement in
advance, and the Republicans, fearing their com-
munications would be cut off, retreated. This is
what I know positively, and from the mouth of a
Republican colonel, wounded in the hip, the second
day of the battle. Doctor Feuerbach, one of my
old university friends, took me to this man. Otherwise, I should have learned nothing reliable, for
one can get nothing but boasts out of the Prussians.
Everybody in the city is talking of these events, but
each in his own manner. Great excitement pre-
vails down there. Convoys of the wounded are constantly leaving for Mayence; the City Hospital is
filled with patients, and the citizens are forced to
receive the wounded into their houses until they can
be removed."

The attention with which Madame Thérèse listened to this recital may be imagined.

" I see—I see," said she, sadly, her head leaning
on her hand. " Our troops were not concentrated
enough."

" Truly they were not; that is what everybody
at Kaiserslautern says; but that doesn't prevent one
from recognizing the courage and even the extraordinary boldness of your Republicans. When they
cried, ' Landau or death! ' in the midst of the firing

of guns, and the roaring of cannon, all the city heard
them; it was enough to make one shudder. Now
they are in retreat, but Brunswick has not dared to
pursue them."

There was a moment's silence, then Madame Thérèse asked:

"And how do you know that our regiment was
not engaged, doctor?"

"From the Republican colonel; he told me that
the first battalion of the second brigade had met
with great losses in a village in the mountain, some
days before, while reconnoitring near Landau, and
that for that reason they were held in reserve. Then
I saw that he understood affairs exactly."

"What is this colonel's name?"

"Pierre Ronsart; he's a tall dark man, with black
hair."

"I know him well—I know him well—he
was captain in our battalion last year; what!
is that poor Ronsart a prisoner? Is his wound
dangerous?"

"No; Feuerbach told me he would recover, but
it will take some time," answered my uncle. Then
smiling archly, his eyes half closed—"Yes, yes—
that's what the colonel told me. But he told me
many other things—interesting things—extraor-

12

dinary things, and which I should never have suspected."

" What were they, doctor? "

" Something that astonished me very much," said Uncle Jacob, pressing the tobacco into his pipe with the end of his finger, and drawing a great puff, looking up at the ceiling—" very much astonished me, and yet not so much—no, not so much either, for such ideas had sometimes come into my head."

" But what is it, Monsieur Jacob? " said Madame Thérèse, in surprise.

" He spoke of a certain *Citoyenne* Thérèse, a sort of Cornelia, known in all the army of the Moselle, and whom the soldiers call ' The *Citoyenne!* ' Ha! ha! ha! It seems that the *citoyenne* doesn't lack a certain courage! " And turning to Lisbeth and me, " Imagine that one day when the leader of their battalion had just been killed in trying to urge on his men, and when a bridge must be crossed which was defended by a battery and two Prussian regiments, and all the oldest Republicans, the most terrible among those courageous men, recoiled—imagine this *Citoyenne* Thérèse taking the flag, and marching all alone across the bridge, telling her little brother Jean to beat the charge before her, as before an army; which produced such an effect upon the Republicans, that they all rushed forward at once, and took the cannons. Do you understand, all of you? It was Colonel Ronsart who told me this."

And as we looked at Madame Thérèse, quite stupefied—I, especially, my eyes wide open,—we saw that she was turning very red.

"Ah," said my uncle, "we learn something new every day; that was grand!—that was fine! Yes, yes, although I am a lover of peace, that moved me very much."

"But, doctor," replied Madame Thérèse, at last, "how could you believe "——

"Oh," interrupted Uncle Jacob, extending his hand, "it wasn't the colonel alone who told me that; two other wounded captains who were there, hearing that *Citoyenne* Thérèse was still living, were greatly rejoiced. The story about her and the flag is known to the lowest soldier. Say—yes or no— did she do that?" said my uncle, frowning, and looking in Madame Thérèse's face.

Then she, drooping her head, began to weep, and said:

"The commander who had just been killed, was our father—we wanted to die, little Jean and I— we were desperate."

As she thought of that, she sobbed. My uncle became very grave, and said:

"Listen, Madame Thérèse: I am proud of having saved the life of such a woman as you. Whether it was because your father had died, or for some other reason, that you acted thus, it was truly grand, noble and courageous. It was even extraordinary, for thousands of other women would only have groaned. They would have become powerless, and done nothing but utter reproaches. But you are a courageous woman, and long after you have performed great actions, you weep when others are beginning to forget. You are not only the woman who lifted up the banner from among the dead, but you are also the woman who weeps, and this is why I esteem you. And I say that the roof of this house in which my father and grandfather once lived, is honored by your presence, yes, honored!"

My uncle spoke gravely, dwelling on the words and placing his pipe on the table, for he was greatly moved. And Madame Thérèse answered: "Doctor, don't speak so, or I shall be obliged to go away. I entreat you not to speak of that again."

"I have told you what I think," replied Uncle Jacob, rising, "and now I will say no more about it, since that is your wish, but that doesn't prevent me from honoring, in you, a gentle and noble creature, and being proud of having taken care of you. And the colonel told me also who your father and brothers were; simple, artless men, who went together to defend what they believed to be justice. When so many thousands of proud men think only of their own interests, and, I say it with regret, when they consider themselves nobles, while thinking only of material things, one likes to see that true nobility, that which comes from disinterestedness and heroism, is found among the people. Let them be Republicans or not, what matters it? I think in my soul and conscience, that the true nobles, in the sight of the Lord, are those who do their duty."

My uncle in his excitement was walking up and down the room, talking to himself. Madame Thérèse, having dried her tears, looked at him smilingly, and said:

"Doctor, you have brought us good news,— thanks—thanks! Now I'm going to get better."

"Yes," replied Uncle Jacob, stopping, "you are going to get better and better. But it is time to rest. We have had much fatigue, and I think we'll all sleep well to-night. Come Fritzel, come Lisbeth, let us go! Good-night, Madame Thérèse."

" Good-night, doctor."

He took the candle, and, with head bent down thoughtfully, followed us upstairs.

XII

THE next day was a day of happiness for Uncle Jacob's house. It was very late when I awoke from my deep sleep; I had slept twelve hours as if it were but a second, and the first things I saw were my little round window-panes, covered with those silver flowers, those transparent nets, and thousand ornaments of frost-work, such as no designer's hand could trace. It is nevertheless but a simple thought of God's, which reminds us of spring in the midst of winter; but it is also the sign of great cold,—of the dry, sharp cold which succeeds snow. Then all the rivers, and even the springs are frozen. The roads are hard, and the pools covered with that white and brittle ice which cracks under the feet like egg-shells. Seeing this with my nose hardly out of the coverlet, and my cotton cap drawn far down over my ears, I recalled all the past winters, and said to myself:

"Fritzel, you won't dare to get up; not even to go to breakfast; you won't dare!"

But a good odor of cream porridge came up from the kitchen, and inspired me with a terrible courage. I had been lying there, thinking, for half an hour, and had just resolved beforehand that I would spring out of bed, take my clothes under my arm, and run down to the kitchen, to dress near the fire, when I heard Uncle Jacob getting up, in his room, next to mine, which led me to think that the great fatigue of the night before had made him as late a sleeper as I. A few minutes afterward he came into my room, laughing and shivering, in his shirt-sleeves.

" Come, come, Fritzel," cried he, " get up, get up! courage! Don't you smell the porridge? "

He always did so in the winter when it was very cold, and amused himself with seeing me in a state of great uncertainty.

" If they could bring the soup here," said I, " I'd smell it much better."

" Oh, the coward, the coward! He would have the heart to eat in bed! What laziness! "

Then, to set me a good example, he poured the cold water from my pitcher into the large basin, and washed his face with both hands, saying:

" This does one good, Fritzel; it freshens you up, and gives you ideas. Come, get up!—Come! "

But I, seeing that he wanted to wash me, sprang from the bed, and with a single bound seized my clothes, and rushed downstairs four steps at a time. My uncle's shouts of laughter filled the house.

" Ah! you'd make a famous Republican, you! " cried he. " Little Jean would have to beat the charge briskly to give you courage! "

But once in the kitchen, I could laugh at his raillery. I was dressing near a good fire, and was bathing with tepid water which Lisbeth poured out for me. That seemed to me much better than having great courage, and I was beginning to contemplate the soup-tureen with an affectionate eye, when Uncle Jacob came down. He pinched my ear, and said to Lisbeth:

" Well, well! how's Madame Thérèse this morning? she has had a good night, I hope? "

" Go in, doctor," replied the old servant, in a good-natured tone; " go in, sir, somebody wants to speak to you."

My uncle entered, and I followed, and we were at first very much surprised to see no one in the sitting-room, and the curtains of the alcove drawn. But our astonishment was very much greater, when, turning round, we saw Madame Thérèse in her cantinière's dress—the little jacket with brass buttons closed to the throat, and the large red scarf around her neck,—seated behind the stove. She looked as we had first seen her, only a little paler. Her hat was on the table, and her beautiful black hair, parted in the middle, fell over her shoulders, making her look like a young man. She was smiling at our astonishment, and kept her hand on the head of Scipio, who was sitting near her.

"Good Lord!" cried my uncle. "How, is it you, Madame Thérèse! You've got up!"

Then he added, anxiously,

"What imprudence!"

But she, continuing to smile, held her hand out to him gratefully, and looking at him expressively with her large black eyes, answered—

"Fear nothing, doctor; I'm well, very well. Your good news of yesterday restored me to health. See, for yourself!"

He took her hand in silence, and felt her pulse thoughtfully. Then his brow cleared, and he cried, in a joyous tone:

"No more fever! Ah now—now, all goes well! But still you must be prudent—be prudent still."

And drawing back he laughed like a child, looking at his patient, who smiled, also.

"I see you again as I saw you first, Madame

Thérèse," he said slowly. " Ah! we've been very fortunate, very fortunate! "

" You've saved my life, Monsieur Jacob," said she, her eyes filled with tears.

But he shook his head and raised his hand—

" No, no, it is He who preserves everything and who animates everything—it is He alone who has saved you; for He does not want all the noble and beautiful natures to perish; He wants some to remain as an example for others. Let us thank Him! "

Then, with voice and countenance changing, he added:

" Let us rejoice! Let us rejoice! This is what I call a happy day! "

He ran into the kitchen, and as he did not return immediately, Madame Thérèse beckoned me to her. She took my head between her hands and kissed me, putting aside my hair.

" You're a good child, Fritzel," said she. " You're like little Jean! "

I was very proud to resemble little Jean.

Then my uncle returned, his eyes twinkling, with an expression of inward satisfaction.

" To-day," said he, " I shan't stir from the house. It is necessary that a man should rest, occasionally. I'm only going to make a little tour of the village,

that I may have a clear conscience, and then I shall
return and pass the whole day with my family, as
I used to do in the good time when grandmother
Lehnel was living. It has well been said that it is
women who make the home."

He put on his large cap, and threw his coat over
his shoulder, and went out, smiling.

Madame Thérèse had become very thoughtful.
She rose, drew her chair to a window, and looked
out upon the square with the fountain, gravely. I
went into the kitchen to breakfast with Scipio. In
about half an hour I heard my uncle come in, saying,

" Well! here I am, free until evening, Madame
Thérèse. I've made my tour: everything's in order, and I'm not obliged to go out again."

Scipio was scratching at the door; I opened it,
and we went into the sitting-room together. My
uncle had just hung his coat on the wall, and was
looking at Madame Thérèse, who was still in the
same place, seeming very melancholy.

" What are you thinking of, Madame Thérèse? "
asked he; " you appear to be sadder than you were
a little while ago."

" I'm thinking, doctor, that in spite of the greatest sufferings, it is pleasant to remain some time

MADAME THERESE HAD BECOME THOUGHTFUL.

longer in this world," said she, in an agitated voice.

" Some time? " cried Uncle Jacob. " Say, rather, for many years; for, thanks to God, you have a good constitution, and in a few days you will be as strong as ever."

" Yes, Monsieur Jacob, yes; I believe it. But when a good man, a kind-hearted man, has raised you from among the dead, at the last moment, it is a very great happiness to feel one's self recovered; to say to one's self, ' But for him, I should not now be living.' "

My uncle then understood that she was contemplating the scene of the terrible battle between her battalion, and the Austrian division; that the old fountain, the tottering walls, the gables, the attic windows—in short, all the small dark square— recalled the incidents of the struggle, and that she knew the fate which awaited her, if he had not fortunately arrived when Joseph Spick was going to throw her into the cart. For a moment he was overwhelmed by this discovery. Then he asked:

" Who told you these things, Madame Thérèse? "

" Yesterday, when you were away, Lisbeth told me how much gratitude I owe you."

" Lisbeth told you that! " cried he, in despair; " yet I had forbidden her."

" Don't reproach her, doctor," said she, " I encouraged her a little. She likes to talk so much! "

She smiled at my uncle, who calmed down immediately, and said:

" Well, well, I ought to have foreseen that—let
us say no more about it. But listen to me,
Madame Thérèse: you must drive such thoughts
from your mind. You must try to look at things
cheerfully; it's necessary to the re-establishment
of your health. All will be well now, but we must
try to assist nature by pleasant thoughts, according
to the precepts of the father of medicine, the wise
Hippocrates—' A strong soul,' said he, ' saves a
weak body! ' The strength of the soul comes from
pleasant, not sad thoughts. I wish this fountain
was at the other end of the village, but since it's
here, and we can't take it away, let us sit by the
stove, so as not to see it any more—that will be
much better."

" I will gladly," said Madame Thérèse, rising.
She leaned on Uncle Jacob's arm; he seemed very
happy to support her. I rolled the arm-chair into
its corner, and we took our places around the fire,
whose crackling gladdened us. At times, in the
distance, we heard a dog bark, and this piercing
sound, which extends so far through the silent coun-

try in very cold weather, awoke Scipio, who got up, and ran toward the door, growling, with bristling moustache, then came back, and stretched himself out near my chair, thinking, no doubt, that a good fire was better than the pleasure of making a noise. Madame Thérèse, pale, with her long blue-black hair falling over her shoulders, seemed calm and happy. We talked quietly, my uncle smoking his porcelain pipe, with an air of gravity, full of satisfaction.

"But tell me, Madame Thérèse," said he, in a few moments, "I thought I cut your jacket, and now it looks as good as new."

"Lisbeth and I mended it yesterday, Monsieur Jacob."

"Ah ! good, good ! Then you know how to sew? That idea hadn't occurred to me before. I've always imagined you on a bridge, or somewhere near a river, under fire."

Madame Thérèse smiled.

"I'm the daughter of a poor school-master," said she, "and the first thing one must do in this world, when one is poor, is to learn how to earn a living. My father knew this ; all his children were taught some trade. It is only a year since we left, and not only our family, but all the young men in the town and surrounding villages, with guns, axes, pitch-forks and scythes—whatever we had—to go and meet the Prussians. Brunswick's proclamation had roused all the frontier. We learned to drill on the way. Then my father, an educated man, was at once chosen captain, by popular vote, and later, after some encounters, he became commander of the battalion. Until our departure, I had helped him with his classes. I took charge of the young girls, and taught them all that good housekeepers ought to know. Ah, Monsieur Jacob, if any one had told me, then, that I should one day march with soldiers, that I should lead my horse by the bridle in the middle of the night, that I should drive my cart over heaps of dead bodies, and often, during whole hours, see my way only by the light of the firing, I would not have believed it ; for I cared only for simple household duties. I was even very timid ; a look would make me blush in spite of myself. But what can we not do when great duties draw us from obscurity, when a country in danger calls her children ! Then the heart bounds, we are no longer the same, we march, fear is forgotten, and long afterward, we are astonished at being so changed, and having done so many things that we would have thought quite impossible ! "

"Yes, yes," said my uncle, bending his head, "now. I understand you—I see things clearly. Ah, it was thus that they rose—it was thus that men marched *en masse!* See what an idea can do!"

We continued talking in this strain until nearly noon, when Lisbeth came to lay the table, and serve dinner. We watched her going and coming, spreading the cloth and placing the dishes, and when she brought the smoking soup, Uncle Jacob said, very gayly:

"Come, Madame Thérèse,"—rising, and helping her to walk—"come to the table. You are now our good grandmother Lehnel, the guardian of the domestic hearth, as my old Professor Eberhardt, of Heidelberg, used to say."

She smiled, too, and when we were seated opposite each other, it seemed to us the natural order of things, that all must have been so ordained from olden times, and that until to-day one of our family had been wanting, whose presence made us happier. Even Lisbeth, bringing in the boiled meat, vegetables and roast, stopped each time to contemplate us with an air of profound satisfaction, and Scipio kept beside me as much as by his mistress, making no difference between us. My uncle helped

13

Madame Thérèse, and as she was still weak, cut her meat for her, saying :

" One more little piece !   What you need now is strength ; eat that too, but then we will stop, for everything ought to be done in moderation."

When we had nearly finished, he went out for a moment, and as I was wondering what he had gone to do, he reappeared with an old bottle with a large red seal, covered with dust.

" There, Madame Thérèse," said he, placing it on the table, " that is one of your fellow-countrymen, who comes to wish you good health.   We cannot refuse him that satisfaction, for he comes from Burgundy, and, they say, has a gay disposition."

" Is this the way you treat your patients, Monsieur Jacob? " asked Madame Thérèse, with emotion.

" Yes, all—I order them whatever will give them pleasure."

" Well, yours is true science—that which comes from the heart, and cures."

My uncle was going to pour out the wine, but stopping suddenly, he looked at the patient with an air of gravity, and said, expressively :

" I see that we agree better and better ; and you will finish by becoming converted to the doctrine of peace."

Then he poured some drops into my glass, and filled his and Madame Thérèse's to the brim, saying:

"To your health, Madame Thérèse!"

"To yours and Fritzel's!"

And we drank that old wine, the color of onion-skin, which I thought very good. We became very gay. Madame Thérèse's cheeks took a slight rose-tint, betokening the return of health. She smiled, and said:

"This wine strengthens me." Then she began to speak of rendering herself useful in the house. "I am already very strong; I can work, I can mend your old linen; you must have some, Monsieur Jacob?"

"Oh, no doubt, no doubt," said my uncle, smiling; "Lisbeth's eyes are not what they were at twenty; she spends hours in darning one hole. You'll be very useful to me, very useful. But it isn't time for that yet. It's still necessary for you to rest."

"But," said she, looking at me sweetly, "if I can't work, yet, you'll at least permit me to take your place for Fritzel, sometimes. You haven't time always to give him your good French lessons, and if you will "——

"Ah, that's different!" cried Uncle Jacob;

" yes, I call that an excellent idea, excellent. Listen, Fritzel : in future you will take your lessons of Madame Thérèse. You must try to profit by them, for good opportunities of instruction are rare —very rare ! "

I had become very red, for I was thinking how much time Madame Thérèse had; but she, guessing my thoughts, said, kindly :

" Don't fear, Fritzel. I'll give you plenty of time for play. We'll read Buffon together, only one hour in the morning, and one at night. Don't be afraid, my child. I won't tire you too much."

She drew me gently to her, and kissed me. Then the door opened, and the mole-catcher and Koffel entered, gravely, dressed in their Sunday clothes. They had come to take coffee with us. It was easy to see that my uncle, on inviting them, in the morning, had told them of the courage and great fame of Madame Thérèse in the armies of the Republic, for they were by no means the same as usual. The mole-catcher no longer kept his fur cap on, and Koffel had put on a white shirt, the collar of which rose above his ears ; he held himself very straight, his hands in his vest pockets, and his wife must have put on a button to fasten the second suspender of his breeches, for they no longer hung upon one side, but

were even on both ; moreover, instead of his old
clogs full of holes, he wore his best shoes.   In short,
both had the appearance of grave personages coming
from some extraordinary conference, and both
bowed very impressively, and said :

"We salute the company ! "

"Good, it's you ! " said my uncle ; "come, sit
down." Then turning toward the kitchen he cried:

"Lisbeth, you may bring the coffee."

At that moment, glancing by chance at the window, he saw old Adam Schmitt passing, and rising
immediately, tapped on the pane, saying :

"Here's an old soldier of Frederic, Madame
Thérèse ; you will be happy to make his acquaintance.   He is a good man."

Father Schmitt had come to see what Uncle Jacob
wanted, and Uncle Jacob, having opened the window, said :

"Father Adam, will you give us the pleasure of
taking coffee with us?   I always have that old cognac, you know ! "

"Willingly, doctor," replied Schmitt, "very
willingly."

Then he appeared in the doorway, and making
the military salute, said :

"Best respects ! "

Then the mole-catcher, Koffel, and Schmitt, standing around the table in embarrassment, began to talk to each other in low tones, looking at Madame Thérèse, as if they had something very important to communicate, while Lisbeth took off the table-cloth, and spread the oil-cloth on, and Madame Thérèse continued to smile upon me, and pass her hand through my hair, without seeming to notice that they were talking about her. At last, Lisbeth brought the cups and the little decanters of cognac and *kirschenwasser* on a tray, and this sight made old Schmitt turn round, his eyes twinkling. Lisbeth brought the coffee-pot, and my uncle said :

" Let us sit down."

Everybody sat down, and Madame Thérèse, smiling on all these honest men, said :

" Allow me to help you, gentlemen."

Immediately, Father Schmitt, again making the salute, answered :

" Military honors to you ! "

Koffel and the mole-catcher looked at him admiringly, and each thought : " That Father Schmitt has just said a sensible and suitable thing."

Madame Thérèse filled the cups, and while they drank in silence, my uncle, placing his hand on Father Schmitt's shoulder, said :

" Madame Thérèse, I present to you an old soldier of Frederic the Great, a man who, notwithstanding his campaigns and his wounds, his courage and his good conduct, became only a simple sergeant, but whom all the honest men in the village esteem as much as a captain."

Then Madame Thérèse looked at Father Schmitt, who straightened himself up in his chair with a feeling of natural dignity.

" In the armies of the Republic, monsieur might have become a general," said she. " If France now fights all Europe, it is because she will not allow that honors, fortune, and all the good things of the world, should crown the heads of a few, despite their vices ; and all the poverty and humiliations the heads of others, notwithstanding their merits and virtues. The nation finds this contrary to the law of God, and to change it, we will all die, if it be necessary ! "

At first no one replied. Schmitt looked at this woman earnestly, his large gray eyes wide open. His lips were compressed, and he seemed to reflect. The mole-catcher and Koffel looked at each other ; Madame Thérèse seemed a little excited, and my uncle remained calm. I had left the table, for Uncle Jacob did not allow me to take coffee, thinking it injurious to children, and was standing behind the stove, looking and listening. In a moment Uncle Jacob said to Schmitt :

"Madame was *cantinière* in the second battalion of the first brigade of the army of the Moselle."

"I know it already, doctor," answered the old soldier ; "and I also know what she did."

Then raising his voice, he cried :

"Yes, madame, if I had had the happiness of serving in the armies of the Republic, I would have become a captain—perhaps even a colonel—or I would have died." Then placing his hand on his breast—"I was ambitious ; not to flatter myself, I wasn't wanting in courage, and if I could have risen I would have been ashamed to remain in an inferior position. The king remarked me on several occasions—a rare thing for a common soldier—and that was an honor. At Rosbach, while the captain behind us cried, ' Forward ! ' it was really Adam Schmitt who commanded the company. Ah, well ! all that amounted to nothing ; and now, although I receive a pension from the King of Prussia, I'm forced to say the Republicans are right. That's my opinion."

Then he emptied his little glass quickly, and winking in an odd manner, added :

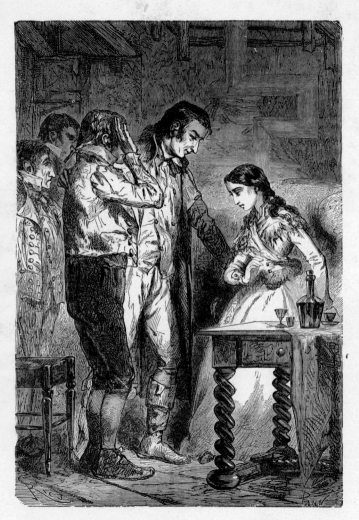

"TO PRESENT YOU MY RESPECTS," SAID OLD SCHMITT.

" And they fight well, I saw that—yes—they fight well. They have not the regular movements of old soldiers, yet, but they sustain a charge well, and it is by that one knows strong men in the ranks."

After these words of Father Schmitt's they all began to praise the new ideas. One would have thought that the signal for a general confidence had just been given, and that each wished to reveal thoughts which he had long kept secret. Koffel, who was always complaining of not having received an education, said that all the children ought to go to school at the country's expense ; that as God had not given more heart and mind to the nobles than to other men, each one had a right to the dew and the light of heaven ; thus the good grain would not be choked by tares, nor the culture which would help more useful plants be wasted upon thistles.

Madame Thérèse replied that the National Convention had voted fifty-four million francs for public education—regretting that they could not do more—at the time when all Europe was in arms against them, and they were obliged to sustain fourteen armies in the field.

Koffel's eyes filled with tears as he heard this, and I shall never forget how he said in a trembling voice—

" Well, God bless them, God bless them ! So much the worse for us, but though I should lose everything through them, it is for their success that I will pray."

The mole-catcher remained silent a long time, but when he once began, there was no stopping him. Not only did he demand education for the children, but he desired the utter overturning of everything. One would not have supposed that so peaceable a man could entertain such ideas.

" I say it's shameful to sell regiments like droves of cattle ! " cried he, earnestly, stretching out his hand over the table.   " I say it's still more shameful to sell the office of judge, for judges, to get their money back, sell justice ;—I say that the Republicans have done well to abolish the convents, in which idleness and all the vices flourish, and everybody ought to be free to go, to come, to trade, to work, to advance in every walk of life, without any one's opposing them.   And, finally, I believe that if the drones won't go, nor work, the good God wants the bees to get rid of them, as we've always seen, and always shall see, until the end of time."

Old Schmitt, then more at his ease, said his ideas were the same as the mole-catcher's and Koffel's ; and my uncle, who until then had preserved his

calmness, could not help approving these senti-
ments, which are the truest, the most natural, and
most just.

"Only," said he, "instead of wanting to do everything in a day, it's much better to work slowly
and progressively. We must employ gentle and
persuasive means, as Christ did. That would be
wiser, and the same results would be obtained."

Madame Thérèse smiled, and said :

"Ah, Monsieur Jacob, no doubt, if everybody
was like you. But for how many hundred years
has Christ preached kindness, justice, and gentleness to men? And yet, do your nobles listen? Do
they treat the peasants like brothers? No, no ! It
is unfortunate, but war is necessary. In the three
years which have just passed, the Republic has done
more for the rights of man than was done in the
eighteen hundred years before. Believe me, doctor, the resignation of good men is a great evil ; it
emboldens the bad, and is productive of no good."

All agreed with Madame Thérèse, and Uncle
Jacob was going to reply, when Clémentz, the carrier, with his large hat covered with oil-cloth, and
his red leather bag, opened the door, and handed in
the newspaper.

"Won't you take some coffee, Clémentz?" said
my uncle.

" No, Monsieur Jacob, thank you, I'm in a hurry; all the letters are late.   Another time."

He went out, and we saw him run past the window.   My uncle opened the paper, and began to read, gravely, the news of that far-off time.   Although very young then, I remember it well.   It seemed to verify the mole-catcher's predictions, and inspired me with intense interest.   The old *Zeitblatt* treated the Republicans as a kind of madmen who had conceived the audacious design of changing the eternal laws of nature.   It recalled, at first, the terrible manner in which Jupiter had overwhelmed the Titans who had revolted against his throne : crushing them under mountains, so that, since then, these unfortunates vomit ashes and flame from the sepulchres of Vesuvius and Etna.   Then it spoke of the melting of the bells stolen from the worship of our fathers and transformed into cannon,—one of the greatest profanations that could be conceived, since what ought to give life to the soul was now destined to kill the body.   It said, also, that the *assignats* were worth nothing, and that soon, when the nobles should again take possession of their châteaux, and the priests of their convents, those valueless papers would be good for nothing but to kindle the kitchen fires.   It charitably warned people to refuse them, no matter at what cost.   After this came the list of executions, and unhappily, it was long ; so the *Zeitblatt* declared that the Republicans had changed the proverb that " wolves do not eat each other."   It laughed at the new era, styled Republican, whose months were called *vendé- miaire, brumaire, frimaire, nivôse, pluviôse*, etc. These madmen intended to change the courses of the stars, and to pervert the seasons, it said ; put winter into summer, and spring into autumn, so that one would no longer know when seed-time or harvest came; they had no common-sense, and all the peasants of France were indignant with them.

So the *Zeitblatt* expressed itself.

Koffel and the mole-catcher glanced at each other gravely, from time to time, during the reading. Madame Thérèse and Father Schmitt seemed very thoughtful ; no one said anything.   My uncle continued to read, stopping a second at each new paragraph, and the old clock went ticking on.

Toward the last, the questions of the war of La Vendée came up, of the taking of Lyons, the occupation of Toulon by the English and Spanish, the invasion of Alsace by Wurmser, and the battle-field of Kaiserslautern, from which these famous Republicans had run like hares.   The *Zeitblatt* predicted that the Republic would come to an end the following spring, and closed by these words of the prophet Jeremiah, which it addressed to the French people :

" Thine own wickedness shall correct thee, and thy backslidings shall reprove thee ; know therefore and see that it is an evil thing and bitter, that thou hast forsaken the Lord thy God."

Then my uncle folded the paper, and said,

" What is one to think of all that? Every day they announce to us that the Republic is near its end ; six months ago it was surrounded on all sides, three quarters of its provinces had risen against it. La Vendée, and we, too, had gained great victories. Well, now it has repulsed us nearly everywhere, it stands against all Europe as a great monarchy could not do; we are no longer in the heart of its provinces, but only on its frontiers; it advances even to our doors, and yet they say it is going to perish ! If it were not the learned doctor Zacharias who writes these things, I should entertain great doubts of their good faith."

" Ah, Monsieur Jacob," replied Madame Thérèse, " perhaps this doctor sees things as he wishes them. That often happens, and does not prevent people from being sincere. They don't wish to deceive, but they deceive themselves."

" As for me," said Father Schmitt, rising, " all
I know is that the Republicans fight well, and if the
French have three or four hundred thousand like
those I've seen, I fear more for ourselves than for
them. That's my opinion. As to Jupiter, who
puts men under Vesuvius to make them vomit fire,
—that's a new kind of battery, that I know nothing
about, but I'd like very well to see it."

" And I," said the mole-catcher, " think that
Doctor Zacharias doesn't know what he is talking
about ; if I edited the paper, I should do otherwise."

He stopped to take a coal from the furnace, for
he felt great need of smoking. Old Schmitt followed his example, and as night had come, they went
out together, Koffel last, pressing Uncle Jacob's
hand and bowing to Madame Thérèse.

XIII

The next day Madame Thérèse occupied herself
with household duties. She visited the presses, un-
folded the table-cloths, towels, and shirts, and even
the old yellow linen which had lain piled up there
since grandmother Lehnel's time. She put aside
what was worth repairing, while Lisbeth placed the
large tub full of ashes in the wash-house. The
water must boil till midnight to make lye for the
great washing. And for several days there was still
more work—washing, drying, ironing, and mending, and all that.

Madame Thérèse had not her equal for needle-
work. This woman, whom people had thought
only fit to pour out glasses of brandy, and jog along
in a cart behind a crowd of *sans-culottes*, knew more
about domestic matters than any gossip in Anstatt.
She even showed us the art of embroidering wreaths,
and of marking the fine linen with red letters, a
thing of which we in the mountains were entirely
ignorant until then, which proves what information

is diffused by great revolutions. Moreover Madame
Thérèse helped Lisbeth in the kitchen, without in-
terfering with her, knowing that the old servants
cannot bear to have their arrangements disturbed.

"You see, Madame Thérèse," the old woman
sometimes said, "how people's notions change. At
first I couldn't endure you on account of your Republic, and now, if you were to go away, I believe
all the house would go, and that we couldn't live
without you."

"Oh," answered she, smiling, "every one has
his own ways. When you did not know me you felt
distrustful of me ; anybody in your place would
have felt the same." Then she added, sadly, "Nevertheless I must go, Lisbeth. My place is not here.
Other duties call me elsewhere."

She was always thinking of her battalion, and
when Lisbeth cried out :

"Pshaw, you must stay with us, you can't leave
us now. You know that they think a great deal of
you in the village ; the people respect you greatly.
Leave your *sans-culottes*. It isn't the life for an
honest person to be struck by balls and other bad
weapons, following the soldiers. We won't let you
go away."

She shook her head, and one could easily see that
14

some day she would say : " To-day, I am going ! "
and that nothing could prevent her.

On the other hand the discussions on war and
peace continued.   It was Uncle Jacob who recommenced them.   Every morning he came down to
convert Madame Thérèse, saying that peace ought
to reign on earth, that in the beginning peace had
been established by God himself, not only among
men, but among animals ; all religions teach the
doctrine of peace ; all sufferings come from war,
pestilence, murder, pillage, incendiarism ; there
must be a chief at the head of governments to main-
tain order, and consequently nobles to support that
chief ; these things had existed in all times; among
the Hebrews, the Egyptians, the Assyrians, the
Greeks and Romans ; the republic of Rome had
understood this; the consuls and dictators were a
kind of kings supported by noble senators, who were
themselves supported by noble knights, who were
above the people.   Such was the natural order, and
it could not be changed without detriment even to
the poorest, for, said he, the poor, in disorder, no
longer find means of gaining a living, and perish like leaves in autumn, when they fall from the
branches which give them sap.   He said many more
things equally strong ; but Madame Thérèse always

found some good reply. She declared that men have equal rights by God's will ; that rank ought to belong to merit, and not to blood ; wise laws, equal for all, establish only equitable differences among citizens, approving the actions of some, and condemning those of others ; it is shameful and miserable to grant honors and authority to those who do not merit them ; it is to degrade authority and honor itself, to cause them to be represented by unworthy persons, and to destroy in all hearts the sentiment of justice by showing that justice does not exist, since everything depends upon the accident of birth ; to establish such a state of things men must be degraded, for intelligent beings would not suffer it ; such degradation is contrary to God's laws ; that we must contend in every way with those who would bring it about for their own profit, and oppose them by all means in our power, even by war,—the most terrible of all, it is true,—but the sin of which falls upon the heads of those who provoke it by trying to establish an everlasting iniquity !

When my uncle heard these replies he would become grave. If he had a journey to take among the mountains, he would mount his horse very thoughtfully, and all day he would seek new and stronger reasons to convince Madame Thérèse. In the evening he would return more cheerful, with proofs which he considered invincible, but his belief did not last long ; for this simple woman, instead of talking about the Greeks and Egyptians, saw at once into the depths of things, and destroyed my uncle's historical proofs by good sense. Yet, Uncle Jacob was not angry ; on the contrary, he exclaimed admiringly :

" What a woman you are, Madame Thérèse ! Without having studied logic, you have a reply for everything. I'd like to see what kind of a face the editor of the *Zeitblatt* would make arguing with you. I'm sure you'd embarrass him, in spite of his great learning and even his good cause ; for ours is the good cause, only I defend it poorly."

Then they would both laugh, and Madame Thérèse would say :

" You defend peace very well. I agree with you ; only let us rid ourselves of those who desire war, and in order to get rid of them, let us wage it better than they. You and I will soon be of one opinion, for we are earnest and desire justice. But there are others who must be converted by cannon-shots, since that is the only voice they will hear, and the only reasoning which they understand."

My uncle would make no answer, and what great

ly astonished me was that he even seemed contented with having been beaten. Next to these great political discussions, that which gave him the most pleasure was to find me, on returning from his visits, taking my French lesson, Madame Thérèse sitting with her arm around me, and I standing, bending over the book. He would come in softly, so as not to disturb us, and sit behind the stove, stretching out his legs, and listening in a sort of rapture. Sometimes he would wait half an hour before taking off his boots and putting on his loose jacket, he was so afraid of distracting my attention ; and when the lesson was finished, he would exclaim :

" Very well, Fritzel, very well ! You're acquiring a taste for that beautiful language that Madame Thérèse explains to you so well. How fortunate for you to have such a teacher ! You'll realize that after a while."

Then he would kiss me, much moved.

What Madame Thérèse did for me he valued more than if it had been for himself.

I must say, also, that that excellent woman did not weary me for a single moment during our lessons ; if she saw my attention lag, she would immediately tell me little stories which aroused me; there was especially a certain Republican Cate-

chism, full of noble and touching incidents, the remembrance of which will never be effaced from my
memory.

Several days passed thus. The mole-catcher and
Koffel came every evening as usual. Madame
Thérèse had entirely recovered, and it seemed as if
this state of things would continue forever, when an
extraordinary occurrence came to disturb our quiet,
and to urge Uncle Jacob to the most daring under-
takings.

XIV

ONE morning Uncle Jacob was gravely reading the Republican Catechism near the stove. Madame Thérèse was sewing by the window, and I was watching for a good opportunity of making my escape with Scipio. Outside our neighbor Spick was splitting wood. No other sound was heard in the village. My uncle's book seemed to interest him very much. From time to time he would look up, and say,

" These Republicans have good traits ; they take a large view of men—their principles elevate the soul. It is really beautiful ! I can understand how the young adopt their doctrines, for all young people who are healthy in body and mind love virtue. Those who become decrepit before they are old, from selfishness and bad passions, are just the opposite. What a pity that such men constantly have recourse to violence ! "

Then Madame Thérèse would smile, and he would resume his reading. This continued for about half an hour, and Lisbeth, after having swept the entry, was going to have her share of gossip at old Rœsel's as usual, when suddenly a man on horseback stopped at our door. He wore a large blue cloth cloak, a sheepskin cap, and had a snub-nose and gray beard. My uncle put down his book. We all looked at the stranger from the windows.

" Somebody has come after you for some sick person, doctor," said Madame Thérèse.

My uncle did not answer. The man, after fastening his horse to the post, entered the house.

" Are you Doctor Jacob? " asked he, opening the door.

" I am he, sir."

" Here is a letter from Doctor Feuerbach of Kaiserslautern."

" Sit down, sir," said Uncle Jacob.

The man remained standing. My uncle became very pale on reading the letter. For a moment he seemed troubled, and looked at Madame Thérèse anxiously.

" I must take back your answer, if there be any," said the man.

" Tell Feuerbach that I thank him,—that is the only answer."

Then without adding anything he went out bare-

headed with the messenger, whom we saw go down
the street, leading his horse toward the inn of the
Little Golden Pitcher. Doubtless he was going to
refresh himself before returning. We saw my uncle pass the window to go into the shed. Then Madame Thérèse seemed disturbed.

"Fritzel," said she, "go take your uncle his
cap."

I went out at once, and found him walking up
and down with long strides before the barn. He
was still holding the letter, not thinking of putting
it in his pocket. Spick was looking at him strange-
ly from his doorway, leaning on his axe. Two or
three of the neighbors, also, were looking from their
windows. It was very cold out-of-doors, and I went
in again. Madame Thérèse had laid down her
work and was sitting pensively with her elbow on
the window-sill. I sat down behind the stove, having no desire to go out again. I remembered all
these things during my childhood ; but what happened afterward, for a long time seemed like a
dream, for I could not understand it. And it is only
since I have grown older, that, thinking it over, I
have understood it. I remember that my uncle
came in a few minutes afterward, saying that men
were scoundrels, creatures who sought only to in-

jure each other ; that he sat down by the little window not far from the door, and began to read his friend Feuerbach's letter ; while Madame Thérèse stood listening to him erect and calm, in her little jacket with its double row of buttons, her hair twisted at the back of her head.

All this I see, and Scipio, too, in the middle of the room, with upturned head and curled up tail. But as the letter was written in Saxon German, all that I could understand of it was that Uncle Jacob had been denounced as a Jacobin, at whose house the rabble of the country assembled to celebrate the Revolution,—that Madame Thérèse was also denounced as a dangerous woman, regretted by the Republicans on account of her extraordinary courage, and that a Prussian officer, accompanied by a sufficient escort, was coming for her the next day, and would send her to Mayence with the other prisoners.   I remember that Feuerbach advised my uncle to be very prudent, because the Prussians, since their victory at Kaiserslautern, were masters of the country, and they were arresting all dangerous men and sending them to Poland, two hundred leagues from there, into the marshes, as an example to others.

What seemed most astonishing to me was the

manner in which Uncle Jacob, the calm man, the great lover of peace, became indignant at his old comrade's advice.   Our little sitting-room, usually so peaceful, was that day the scene of a terrible storm, and I doubt whether it had ever seen the like, since the house was built.   My uncle accused Feuerbach of being a self-seeker, ready to bow to the arrogance of the Prussians, who treated the Palatinate and the Hundsruck like a conquered country.   He declared that laws existed in Mayence, in Trèves and Spire, as well as in France ; Madame Thérèse had been left for dead by the Austrians ; they had no right to reclaim persons and things which they had abandoned ; she was free ; he would suffer no one to lay his hand on her ; he would protest against it ; the lawyer Pfeffel of Heidelberg was his friend; he would write, he would defend himself ; he would move heaven and earth ; they should see if Jacob Wagner would allow himself to be treated in that manner; they would be astonished at what a peaceable man was capable of doing for right and justice.

As he talked he walked up and down with disordered hair ; he quoted at random in Latin all the old laws that he could recall.   He also spoke of certain sentences on the rights of man which he had just read, and from time to time he stopped, bent his knee, put his foot down with force, and cried :

"I stand on the basis of law—on the brazen foundations of our ancient charters. Let the Prussians come—let them come ! This woman is mine —I rescued her and saved her life. The thing abandoned, '*res derelicta est res publica, res vulgata.*'"

I do not know where he had learned all this ; perhaps at the University of Heidelberg, hearing his companions argue among themselves. But at that time all these old studies passed through his mind and he seemed to be replying to a dozen persons who were attacking him at once.

Madame Thérèse remained calm, her long, thin face very thoughtful. No doubt my uncle's quotations astonished her, but seeing things clearly, as usual, she understood her true position. It was only at the end of a long half-hour, when my uncle opened his secretary and seated himself to write to the lawyer Pfeffel, that she placed her hand gently on his shoulder, and said with emotion :

"Don't write, Monsieur Jacob, it is useless. Before your letter arrives I shall be far away."

My uncle looked at her, turning very pale.

"You want to go away, then?" he asked with trembling lips.

"I am a prisoner," said she, "I know that; my only hope was that the Republicans, returning to the attack, would deliver me as they marched upon Landau; but since it is otherwise, I must go."

"You want to go away!" repeated he, despairingly.

"Yes, doctor, I want to go, to spare you great annoyance; you are too good, too generous to understand the strict laws of war; you see only justice! But in time of war, justice is nothing, force is everything. The Prussians are conquerors, they will come and take me away because those are their orders. Soldiers know only their orders; law, life, honor, man's reason, are nothing; their orders are above all."

My uncle sank back in his arm-chair, his large eyes filled with tears, not knowing what to reply; but he took Madame Thérèse's hand, and pressed it with great emotion, then rising with agitated face, he began to walk up and down, again invoking the execration of future ages upon the oppressors of mankind, cursing Richter and all scoundrels like him, and declaring in a voice of thunder that the Republicans were right in defending themselves; their cause was just; he saw it now; and all the old laws, the old rubbish of ordinances, rules and charters of all sorts had never benefited any but the nobles and monks, to the injury of the poor. His face was swollen, he staggered, he could no longer speak plainly, but stammered. He said that everything ought to be wholly abolished ; courage and virtue only ought to triumph, and finally, in an extraordinary kind of enthusiasm, his arm extended toward Madame Thérèse, and his face red even to his neck, he proposed to take her in his sleigh to the mountain, to the house of a woodcutter—one of his friends—where she would be safe. He seized her hands, and said :

" Let us go—let us go there—you will be well cared for in old Ganglof's house. He is entirely devoted to me—I saved his life, and his son's—they will conceal you—the Prussians will not go look for you in the passes of the Lauterfelz ! "

But Madame Thérèse refused, saying that if the Prussians should not find her at Anstatt, they would arrest him in her place; and she would rather risk perishing of fatigue and cold on the highway, than expose to such a misfortune, a man who had rescued her from among the dead. She said this very firmly, but my uncle would give no weight to such reasons. I remember that what troubled him most was the thought of seeing Madame Thérèse going away with barbarous men, savages from the depths of Pomerania ; he could not endure this idea, and cried :

"You are weak—you are still an invalid ! These Prussians respect nothing—they are a race full of boasting and brutality. You don't know how they treat their prisoners. I have seen it myself—it is a disgrace to my country—I would have concealed this, but I must acknowledge it now, it is frightful!"

"No doubt, Monsieur Jacob," replied she ; "I know that from the old prisoners of our battalion. We shall march two by two, or four by four, sad, sometimes without bread, often hurried and brutally treated by the escort. But your peasants are good —they are honest men—they have pity—and the French are gay, doctor,—the journey will be the only hardship ; and moreover I shall find ten, twenty of my comrades to carry my little bundle ; the French respect women. I see it beforehand," said she, smiling sadly : "one of us will march before, singing an old air of Auvergne to mark the step, or else a more joyous Provençal song, to brighten your dark skies. We shall not be so unhappy as you think, Monsieur Jacob."

She spoke gently, her voice trembling a little, and as she was speaking I could see her with her little

bundle in the file of prisoners, and my heart sank.
Oh, then I knew how much we loved her, how it
would pain us to see her go away.   Suddenly I burst
into tears, and my uncle sitting opposite the secretary, his face in his hands, remained silent, but great
tears flowed slowly down his cheeks.   Madame Thérèse, seeing this, could not help weeping.   She
took me tenderly in her arms, and kissed me warmly,
saying :

"Don't cry, Fritzel; don't cry so.   You'll think
of me sometimes—won't you?   I shall never forget
you."

Scipio alone remained calm, walking around the
stove, and understanding nothing of our trouble.
It was not until nearly ten o'clock, when we heard
Lisbeth lighting the kitchen fire, that we became
somewhat calm.

Then my uncle, blowing his nose forcibly, said :

"Madame Thérèse, you must go, since you really
wish to, but it is impossible for me to allow the Prussians to come here and take you away like a thief,
and lead you through the whole village.   If one of
those brutes should speak a cruel or insolent word to
you, I should forget myself, for my patience would
be at an end ; I feel it, I should be capable of pro-
ceeding to great extremities.   Let me take you to

Kaiserslautern myself, before those people come. We will leave early in the morning, between four and five o'clock, in my sleigh ; we will take the by-roads, and will get down there by noon at the latest. Do you consent? "

" Oh, Monsieur Jacob, how could I refuse this last proof of your affection? " said she, much moved. " I accept it with gratitude."

" We will do so, then," said he gravely. " And now let us dry our tears, and drive away these bitter thoughts as much as possible, so as not to sadden the last moments that we shall spend together."

He kissed me, putting back the hair from my forehead, and said:

" Fritzel, you're a good child; you have an excellent heart. Remember that your Uncle Jacob has been satisfied with you this day. It is good to say to ourselves that we have given satisfaction to those who love us! "

15

XV

From that moment quiet returned to our house. Every one thought of Madame Thérèse's departure, of the great void that would be left in our home, of the sadness which would for weeks and months succeed the pleasant evenings that we had passed together, of the sorrow of the mole-catcher, Koffel, and old Schmitt, on learning the bad news; the more we thought of it, the more causes for grief and loneliness we discovered. What seemed to me the most bitter, was parting from my friend Scipio. I dared not say it, but when I considered that he was going away, that I could no longer walk with him in the village, in the midst of universal admiration, nor have the happiness of making him drill— that I should be as I was before he came, walking alone, my hands in my pockets, and my cotton cap drawn over my ears, without honor, and without glory—such a disaster seemed to me the height of misery. And what caused the bitter cup to overflow, was that Scipio had just placed himself before me, looking at me from under his frowsy eyebrows, as sorrowfully as if he understood that we were going to be separated forever. Oh, when I think of these things even now, I am surprised that my thick, fair curls did not turn quite gray, in the midst of such distracting thoughts. I could not even cry, my sorrow was so great. I remained with head upturned, my lips trembling, and my hands clasped around one knee.

My uncle was walking up and down with long strides, and occasionally he coughed a little, and then quickened his steps.

Madame Thérèse, always active, despite her sadness, and her red eyes, had opened the chest of old linen, and was cutting from thick cloth a kind of bag with double straps, in which to put her things for the journey. We could hear the crunching of her scissors on the table. She arranged the pieces with her usual skill. At last, when all was ready, she drew from her pocket a needle and thread, sat down, put on her thimble, and after that we could see her hand coming and going like lightning. This was all done in the greatest silence. We heard only my uncle's heavy step on the floor, and the measured ticking of our old clock, which neither our joys nor our sorrows could hasten or delay one second. Thus goes life;—time as it passes does not ask, "Are you sad? Are you gay? Do you weep? Do you laugh? Is it spring, autumn, or winter?" It goes on, goes on, always; and those millions of atoms that whirl about in a ray of sunlight, and whose life begins and ends from one "tic-tac" to another, are of as much account to it, as the existence of an old man of a hundred years. Alas! we are but trifles.

Lisbeth having come in toward noon to lay the cloth, my uncle stopped his walk, and said:

"You must cook a little ham for to-morrow morning. Madame Thérèse is going away."

And as the old woman looked at him in amazement—

"The Prussians claim her as their prisoner," said he, in a hoarse voice; "they have force on their side; they must be obeyed."

Then Lisbeth put her plates on the table, and looking from one to the other, settled her cap as if this news had disarranged it, and said:

"Madame Thérèse going away?—that isn't possible—I'll never believe that!"

"It's necessary, my poor Lisbeth," replied Madame Thérèse, sadly; "it's necessary; I'm a prisoner—they are coming to look for me."

" The Prussians? "

" Yes, the Prussians."

Then the old woman, choking with anger, said:

" I always thought the Prussians were no great things—a heap of scoundrels—real ruffians! Coming to attack an honest woman! If men had two farthings' worth of heart, would they suffer it? "

" And what would you do? " asked Uncle Jacob, his face lighting up, for the old servant's indignation secretly pleased him.

" I? I'd load my cavalry pistol," cried Lisbeth, " and call to them through the window, ' Leave, ruffians! don't come in here, or beware! ' And the first one who should pass through the door, I'd stretch out, stiff. Oh, the wretches! "

" Yes, yes," said my uncle, " that's the treatment such men ought to receive. But we're not the strongest."

Then he resumed his walk, and Lisbeth, trembling all over, arranged the dishes. We ate our dinner very silently. When we had finished, my uncle went to get a bottle of old Burgundy from the cellar, and came back, saying sadly,

" Let us rejoice our hearts a little, and fortify ourselves against these great sorrows which overwhelm us. Before your departure let this old wine

which has strengthened you, Madame Thérèse, and
gladdened us all with a day of happiness, sparkle
again in our midst like a ray of sunlight, and scatter
for a few moments the clouds that surround us."

As he said this, in a firm voice, we for the first
time recovered our courage a little. But when, a
few minutes after, he told Lisbeth to get a glass
to drink with Madame Thérèse, and the poor old
woman burst into tears, with her face in her apron,
our firmness vanished, and we all cried together in
great distress.

" Yes, yes," said Uncle Jacob, " we have been
very happy together—such is the life of man—joyful moments pass quickly, and sorrow lasts long.
He who looks down upon us from above knows,
nevertheless, that we do not deserve to suffer thus;
that wicked men have made us miserable; but He
knows, also, that power, true power is in His hand,
and that He can make us happy whenever He
wishes. This is why He permits these iniquities—
He will reward us. Then let us be calm and trust
in Him. To the health of Madame Thérèse! "

And we all drank, the tears running down our
cheeks. Lisbeth, hearing the power of God men-
tioned, was somewhat quieted, for she was pious,
and thought that things ought to be as they are,

I'VE ALWAYS THOUGHT THESE PRUSSIANS DIDN'T AMOUNT TO MUCH.

for the greatest good of all in the life eternal, but she did not the less continue to curse the Prussians, and all who were like them, from the bottom of her soul.

After dinner my uncle charged her particularly not to tell of what was going to happen in the village, for if she did, Richter, and all the bad men in Anstatt, would be there the next day to see Madame Thérèse depart, and to rejoice in our humiliation. She understood him very well, and promised to be discreet. Then my uncle went to see the mole-catcher. All that afternoon I did not leave the house. Madame Thérèse continued her preparations for departure. Lisbeth helped her, and wanted to crowd into her bag a quantity of useless things, saying that all would be needed on the way —one is glad to find what one has put in a corner; that having gone to Pirmasens one day she missed her comb and braided ribbons very much.

Madame Thérèse smiled.

" No, Lisbeth," said she, " remember that I'm not going to travel in a carriage, and that I have to carry everything on my back. Three good chemises, three handkerchiefs, two pairs of shoes, and a few pairs of stockings are enough. At every halting-place we stop an hour or two at the spring, and do our washing. You don't know what a soldier's washing is? How many times I have done it! We French like to be neat, and we are so, with our little bundle."

She seemed cheerful, and it was only when she occasionally addressed some friendly words to Scipio that her voice became very sad. I did not know why, but I knew later, when Uncle Jacob returned. The day wore on. At four o'clock night began to fall. All was now ready; the bag containing Madame Thérèse's things hung on the wall. She sat down by the stove, taking me on her lap in silence. Lisbeth went into the kitchen to prepare supper, and after that not a word was spoken. The poor woman was doubtless thinking of the future which awaited her on her way to Mayence, in the midst of her companions in misfortune. She said nothing, and I felt her sweet breath on my cheek.

Half an hour afterward, when it was quite dark, my uncle opened the door, and asked:

"Are you there, Madame Thérèse?"

"Yes, doctor."

"Good, good! I've been to see my patients— I've told Koffel, the mole-catcher, and old Schmitt. All's right—they'll be here this evening to receive your adieux."

His voice was firm. He went into the kitchen to get a light, and returning, seemed much pleased to see us together.

"Fritzel behaves well," said he. "Now he is going to lose your good lessons; but I hope he will practise reading French alone, and remember always that a man is worthy only in proportion to his knowledge. I rely upon that."

Then Madame Thérèse made him examine her little bag in detail. She smiled, and my uncle said:

"What happy dispositions the French have. In the midst of the greatest misfortunes they preserve a store of natural gayety; their sorrow never lasts many days. That is what I call a gift from God, the finest, the most desirable of all."

But on that day,—the remembrance of which will never be effaced from my memory, because it was the first time I had witnessed the unhappiness of those I loved,—in all that day, what touched me most, was this:—a little while after supper, Madame Thérèse, sitting quietly behind the stove, Scipio's head on her knees, looking dreamily before her, said suddenly:

"Doctor, I owe you much—and yet I must ask one more favor of you."

" What is it, Madame Thérèse? "

" It is that you will take care of my poor Scipio —take care of him, in remembrance of me. Let him be Fritzel's companion, as he has been mine, that he may not have to endure the new trials of a prisoner's life."

When she said that, I felt my heart swell, and I trembled all over with delight and tenderness. I was sitting on my little low chair before the fire. I drew my Scipio to me, and plunged my two coarse red hands into his thick hair; a flood of tears rushed down my face. It seemed to me that I had lost all the blessings of heaven and earth, and they had just been restored to me.

My uncle looked at me in surprise. He must have understood what I had suffered at the thought of being separated from Scipio, for instead of speaking to Madame Thérèse of the sacrifice which she was making, he said, simply:

" I accept, Madame Thérèse, I accept for Fritzel, that he may remember how much you loved him; that he may always recollect that in your greatest sorrow you left him, as a mark of your affection, a good faithful creature,—not only your own companion, but little Jean's, your brother's, also. Let him never forget it, and love you too."

Then turning to me:

"Fritzel, don't you thank Madame Thérèse?"

I got up, and not being able to say a word, from sobbing, threw myself into that excellent woman's arms, where I remained, my arm on her shoulder, looking through great tears at Scipio, who was at our feet, and touching him with my finger-ends, with an unspeakable joy. It was some time before I could be quieted. Madame Thérèse kissed me, saying:

"This child has a good heart. He becomes attached to one easily—that is good!" which increased my tears. She smoothed the hair from my forehead, and seemed moved.

After supper, Koffel, the mole-catcher, and old Schmitt came in, their caps under their arms. They expressed to Madame Thérèse their grief at parting from her, and their indignation against that scoundrel, Richter, to whom everybody attributed the denunciation, for he alone was capable of such an act. They sat around the stove. Madame Thérèse was touched with the sorrow of these honest people, but nevertheless her firmness and decision did not desert her.

"Listen, my friends," said she: "if the world were strewn with roses, and if we found every-

where only noble men to celebrate justice and right,
what merit would there be in advocating these principles? Really, it would not be worth the trouble of
living. We happen to live in times in which great
things are done, when liberty is fought for. We
shall at least be remembered, and our existence will
not have been useless; all our poverty, all our sufferings, all the blood which we have shed will form
a sublime spectacle for future generations; wicked
men will quake when they think that they might
have encountered and been swept away by us, and
all great souls will regret not having been alive to
share our labors. These are the teachings of events.
Do not pity me then. I am proud and happy to
suffer for France, who represents liberty, right, and
justice, in the world. You believe us beaten?
That is a mistake. We retreated one step yesterday; we will take twenty steps forward to-morrow.
And if France one day is so unfortunate as no longer
to represent the great cause that we defend, other
people will take our places, and carry on our work,
for justice and freedom are immortal, and all the
despots in the world will never succeed in destroy-
ing them. As for me, I may go to Mayence, and
perhaps to Prussia, escorted by Brunswick's soldiers; but remember what I say to you: the Re-

publicans have made only their first day's march, and I am sure that before the close of next year they will come to deliver me."

Thus spoke this proud woman, smiling, with flashing eyes. We could easily see that suffering was nothing to her, and each one thought, "If these are the Republican women, what must the men be?"

Koffel grew pale with pleasure, as he listened to her. The mole-catcher winked at my uncle, and said, very low:

"I've known all that a long time; it's written in my book. These things must happen—it's written!"

Old Schmitt, having asked permission to light his pipe, blew great puffs, one after another, and murmured between his teeth:

"How unfortunate that I'm not twenty years old! I would join those people! That's what I'd do. What could prevent me from becoming a general, like any other man? How unfortunate!"

At nine o'clock my uncle said:

"It's late. We must leave before day. I think we had better take a little rest."

And everybody rose with emotion. They kissed like old friends, promising never to forget each other. Koffel and Schmitt went out first; the mole-catcher and my uncle stopped a moment in the doorway, talking in low tones. The moonlight was superb, the earth was all white, the sky of a dark-blue, crowded with stars. Madame Thérèse, Scipio, and I went out together to see this magnificent sight, which makes one feel the littleness and vanity of human beings, and overwhelms the mind with its illimitable grandeur.

Then the mole-catcher went away, pressing my uncle's hand again. We saw him as if it were broad daylight, walking down the deserted street. At last he disappeared at the corner of Orties Lane, and as it was very cold, we all went in to say good-night.

My uncle kissed me at the door of my chamber, and said in a strange voice, pressing me to his heart—

" Fritzel—work—work—and behave well, dear child! "

He went into his room, much agitated.

For my part, I could only think of the happiness of taking care of Scipio. Once in my room, I put him on the bed, at my feet, between the warm feather bed and the bedstead. He lay quiet, with his head between his paws. I could feel his sides dilate gently at every breath, and I would not have changed places with the Emperor of Germany. I could not sleep until after ten o'clock, for thinking of my happiness. My uncle was moving about in his room. I heard him open his secretary and afterward make a fire in his chamber stove for the first time that winter, and I thought he intended to sit up. At last I slept soundly.

XVI

THE church-clock was striking nine when I was
awakened by a clattering of hoofs before our house;
horses were stamping on the hard ground, and I
heard people talking at our door. It immediately
occurred to me that the Prussians had come to take
Madame Thérèse, and I hoped with all my heart
that Uncle Jacob had not slept as long as I had.
Two minutes afterward I went downstairs, and
found at the entrance five or six hussars wrapped
in their cloaks, great scabbards hanging below their
stirrups, and swords in their hands. The officer, a
small, thin, fair man, with hollow cheeks, prominent cheek-bones, and thick reddish moustaches,
was seated on a great black horse, and Lisbeth,
broom in hand, was replying to his questions with a
frightened air. Farther off, was a group of people,
open-mouthed, pressing eagerly forward to listen.
Among the foremost, I noticed the mole-catcher,
his hands in his pockets, and M. Richter, who was
smiling, half-closing his eyes, and showing his

teeth like a happy old fox. He had come, no doubt, to enjoy my uncle's confusion.

" So your master and the prisoner went away together this morning?" said the officer.

" Yes, *monsieur le commandant*," answered Lisbeth.

" At what hour?"

" Between five and six, *monsieur le commandant*; it was still dark. I fastened the lantern to the pole of the sleigh."

" You had heard we were coming, then?" said the officer, giving her a piercing glance.

Lisbeth looked at the mole-catcher, who came out from the circle, and answered, for her, without hesitation:

" I beg your pardon, sir, I saw Dr. Jacob last evening—he's one of my friends. This poor woman knows nothing about it. The doctor has been tired of the Frenchwoman for a long time, he wanted to get rid of her, and when he saw that she could bear the journey he profited by the first moment."

" But why did we not meet them on the way?" cried the Prussian, scanning the mole-catcher from head to foot.

" You must have taken the valley road; the doc-

16

tor went, perhaps, by the way of Waldeck and the mountain. There's more than one road to Kaiserslautern."

The officer, without replying, sprang from his horse, entered our room, pushed open the kitchen door, and pretended to look round; then he came out and said, as he mounted his horse—

" Come, our work is done; the rest doesn't concern us."

He rode toward the Little Golden Pitcher; his men followed, and the crowd dispersed, talking over these wonderful occurrences. Richter seemed confused and angry, and Spick looked at us askance. They went up the steps of the inn together, and Scipio, who was on our steps, ran out, barking at them with all his might.

The hussars refreshed themselves at the Little Golden Pitcher, then we saw them pass our house again on the road to Kaiserslautern, and after that we heard no more of them.

Lisbeth and I thought my uncle would return at night, but when that day passed, and the next, and the next, without our even receiving a letter, our anxiety may be imagined. Scipio went up and down the house, and thrust his nose, from morning till evening, in at the bottom of the door, calling

Madame Thérèse, snuffing, and crying in a lamentable way. His sorrow infected us. A thousand thoughts of misfortune came into our minds. The mole-catcher came to see us every evening, and said:

" There's nothing to be frightened about. The doctor wanted to protect Madame Thérèse; he couldn't let her go with the prisoners, that would be contrary to good sense; he has asked an audience of Field Marshal Brunswick to try to induce him to allow her to enter the hospital of Kaiserslautern. All these steps take time,—be calm; he'll come back."

These words would reassure us a little, for the mole-catcher seemed very calm. He smoked his pipe by the stove, with outstretched legs, and dreamy face.

Unfortunately the forest-guard, Rœdig, who lived in the wood on the road from Pirmasens, where the French then were, had just brought a report to the mayoralty of Anstatt, and having stopped a few minutes at Spick's inn, he said Uncle Jacob had passed his house three days before, about eight o'clock in the morning, and he and Madame Thérèse had even stopped a moment to warm themselves and drink a glass of wine. He said my uncle seemed in very good spirits, and had two long cavalry pistols in his overcoat pockets.

Then the report spread that Uncle Jacob, instead of going to Kaiserslautern, had conducted the prisoner to the Republicans, and that caused great scandal. Richter and Spick declared, everywhere, that he deserved to be shot; that it was an abomination, and his property must be confiscated. The mole-catcher and Koffel answered that the doctor had no doubt lost his way on account of the great snow; that he had taken the mountain road to the left instead of turning to the right; but everybody knew very well that Uncle Jacob was more familiar with the country than any smuggler, and the indignation increased daily. I could no longer go out without hearing my companions say that Uncle Jacob was a Jacobin; and I had to fight in his defence, and despite Scipio's assistance, I came home more than once with a bloody nose.

Lisbeth was in despair, especially at the threats of confiscation.

"What a misfortune!" said she, clasping her hands; "what a misfortune to be forced, at my age, to take my bundle and leave a house where half of my life has been passed!"

It was very sad. The mole-catcher alone preserved his tranquillity.

"You are crazy to fret so," said he; "I tell you Dr. Jacob is well, and that they will confiscate nothing. Keep yourself quiet, eat well, sleep well, and I'll answer for the rest."

He winked mischievously, and always ended by saying:

"My book relates these things. Now they are being accomplished, and all will be well."

Notwithstanding these assurances things went from bad to worse, and the rabble of the village, excited by the scoundrel Richter, were beginning to shout under our windows, when one fine morning, order was suddenly restored. Toward evening the mole-catcher arrived, with a very joyous face, and took his usual place, saying to Lisbeth, who was spinning:

"Well, they don't shout any more, they no longer wish to confiscate; they keep very quiet, ha! ha! ha!"

He said no more, but in the night we heard many carriages passing, and men marching in crowds through the main street. It was worse than the arrival of the Republicans, for no one stopped —they went on and on always! I could not sleep, for Scipio growled every minute. At daybreak, I looked out of the window, and saw half a score more of large wagons, full of wounded men, jolting along in the distance. It was the Prussians. Then came two or three cannon, then a hundred hussars, cuirassiers, dragoons, pell-mell, in great disorder; then dismounted horsemen, carrying their cloak-bags on their shoulders, and covered with mud. They all seemed tired; but they did not stop, nor go into any of the houses, but marched as if the devil were at their heels.

The people, standing at their doors, watched them sullenly. Looking toward the Birkenwald, we could see the files of ambulances, wagons, cavalry and infantry, stretching beyond the forest. It was Field Marshal Brunswick's army in retreat after the battle of Froeschwiller—as we learned later. It had passed through the village in a single night; that was from the 28th to the 29th of December, if I remember rightly; it was early in the next day that the mole-catcher and Koffel arrived in high spirits; they had a letter from Uncle Jacob; and the mole-catcher, showing it to us, said:

"Ha! ha! ha! this is good—this is good! the reign of justice and equality is beginning! Listen awhile!"

He sat down by the table, spreading out his elbows. I stood near him, and read over his shoulder,

BATTLE OF FROESCHWILLER.

Lisbeth was behind me, very pale, and Koffel, leaning against the cupboard, smiling and stroking his chin. They had already read the letter two or three times, and the mole-catcher knew it nearly by heart.

He read what follows, stopping sometimes to look at us with enthusiasm:

WISSEMBOURG, 8th NIVOSE, 2nd YEAR
OF THE FRENCH REPUBLIC.

" *To the Citizens Mole-catcher, and Koffel; to the Citoyenne Lisbeth; to the little Citizen Fritzel, greeting and fraternity!*

" Citoyenne Thérèse and I wish you joy, peace, and prosperity.

" You will know by this that we are writing these lines at Wissembourg in the midst of the triumphs of war. We drove the Prussians from Froeschwiller, and fell like a thunderbolt on the Austrians at Geisberg. Thus pride and presumption are receiving their reward. When people will not listen to good reasons, we must give them better ones; but it is terrible to go to such extremities; yes, it is terrible!

" My dear friends, for a long time I groaned inwardly at the blindness of those who rule the dynasties of old Germany. I deplored their unjust spirit, their egotism. I asked myself if it were not my duty as an honest man to break away from these arrogant creatures, and adopt the principles of justice, equality, and fraternity, proclaimed by the French Revolution. This threw me into great trouble, for a man clings to the ideas that he has received from his ancestors, and such internal changes are not made without great suffering. Still I hesitated, but when the Prussians, contrary to the laws of nations, claimed the unfortunate prisoner whom I had saved, I could bear it no longer. I immediately resolved to take her to Pirmasens, instead of Kaiserslautern—which I have done with the help of God. At three o'clock in the afternoon we came in sight of the outposts, and as Madame Thérèse looked out, she heard the drum, and cried: ' These are the French! Doctor, you have deceived me! ' She threw herself into my arms, and burst into tears, and I, too, began to weep—I was so much moved!

" All along the route from *Trois-Maisons* to the square of the Temple-Neuf, the soldiers shouted, ' Here's *Citoyenne* Thérèse! ' They followed us, and when we got out of the sleigh, several embraced me with true feeling. Others pressed my hands—in fact they overwhelmed me with honors.

" I will not tell you, my dear friends, of the meeting between Madame Thérèse and little Jean; such scenes cannot be described! All the veterans of the battalion, even Colonel Duchêne, who is not soft-hearted, turned their heads to conceal their tears. It was such a sight as I had never seen in my life. Little Jean is a good boy; he resembles my dear little Fritzel very much, so I love him dearly.

" That day extraordinary events occurred at Pirmasens. The Republicans were encamped around the city. General Hoche announced that they were going into winter quarters, and ordered them to build barracks. But the soldiers refused; they wanted to lodge in the houses. Then the general declared that those who refused this service, should not march to battle. I was present at this proclamation, which was read to the companies, and saw General Hoche forced to pardon the men, in front of the prince's palace, for they were in the greatest despair.

" The general having learned that a physician from Anstatt had brought *Citoyenne* Thérèse back to the first battalion of the second brigade, I received an order about eight o'clock to go to the Orangery. Then I found the general standing near a deal table, dressed like a simple captain, with two other citizens, whom I was told, were members of the convention, Lacoste and Baudot, two large, lank men, who looked at me askance. The general is a dark man, with golden-brown eyes, and hair parted in the middle. He came forward and looked at me a few seconds. I, remembering that this young man commanded the army of the Moselle, felt troubled; but suddenly he extended his hand to me, and said, ' Doctor Wagner, I thank you for what you have done for Madame Thérèse; you are a good-hearted man.'

" Then he led me to the table on which a map was spread out, and made various inquiries about the country, so intelligently, that one would have thought he knew more about it than I. I naturally replied, the others listening in silence. Finally he said: ' Doctor Wagner, I cannot propose to you to serve in the armies of the Republic; your nationality prevents that; but the first battalion of the second brigade has just lost its chief surgeon; the service of our ambulances is now incomplete; we have only young men to care for the wounded—I confide this post of honor to you—humanity knows no country! Here is your commission.' He wrote some words at the end of the table, and then took my hand again, saying: 'Doctor, believe that I esteem you! ' Then I went away.

"Madame Thérèse awaited me outside; you can conceive her joy, when she heard that I was to have charge of the ambulance department of the battalion.

"We expected to remain at Pirmasens until spring, and the barracks were being built, when on the next night but one, about ten o'clock, we suddenly received orders to march, without putting out the fires, without making any noise, without beating the drums or sounding the trumpet. All Pirmasens was asleep. I had two horses, riding one, and leading the other, and was in the midst of officers near Colonel Duchêne.

"We left, some on horseback, others on foot, cannon, wagons, ambulances in our midst, flanked by the cavalry, with no moon or anything to guide us. Only from time to time a horseman would cry at the turning of the road 'This way!—this way! ' Toward eleven the moon came out; we were in the midst of the mountains; all the peaks were white with snow. The foot soldiers, with their guns on their shoulders, ran to warm themselves. Two or three times I was obliged to dismount, I was so benumbed. Madame Thérèse, in her cart, covered with gray cloth, handed me the bottle, and the captains were always on hand to receive it after me; more than one soldier, also, had his turn.

"But we went on, on, without stopping, so that about six o'clock, when the pale sun began to brighten the sky,

we had reached Lembach, under the great wooded declivity of Steinfelz, three quarters of a league from
Wœrth. Then was heard on all sides, the command,
'Halt! halt!' Those in the rear were constantly coming; at half-past six all the army was reunited in a valley, and set to work to make soup.

"General Hoche, whom I saw pass with his two tall
members of the Convention, was laughing; he seemed in
a good humor. He went into the last house in the village. The people were as astonished to see us at that
hour, as those in Anstatt were at the arrival of the Republicans. The houses here are so small and miserable,
that it was necessary to take two tables out of doors, and
the general held his council with the officers in the open
air, while the troops cooked the provisions they had
brought. This halt lasted only long enough for us to
eat, and buckle on our knapsacks again. Then we resumed our march in better order. At eight o'clock, on
coming out of the valley of Reichshofen, we saw the
Prussians intrenched on the heights of Froeschwiller
and Wœrth. They were more than twenty thousand
strong, and their redoubts rose one above the other.

"All our army understood that we had marched so
quickly in order to surprise the Prussians alone, for the
Austrians were four or five leagues from there, on the
line of the Motter. But I cannot conceal from you, my
dear friends, that this sight gave me, at first, a terrible
shock. The more I saw, the more impossible it seemed
to me that we should gain the battle. In the first place,
they were more numerous than we; then they had dug
ditches intrenched with palisades, and behind them one

could easily see the gunners, who were leaning over
their cannon and watching us, while files of innumerable
bayonets stretched clear up the side of the hill.

" The French, with their careless natures, saw nothing of this, and even seemed very joyous. The report
was spread that General Hoche had just promised six
hundred francs for every piece taken from the enemy;
they were laughing, putting their hats on one side,
looking at the cannons, and shouting—' Going! Gone! '
It made one shiver to see such indifference, and hear
these pleasantries. The rest of us, the ambulances, the
vehicles of all sorts, the empty wagons for transporting
the wounded, remained in the rear; and to tell the truth,
that gave me real pleasure. Madame Thérèse was thirty
or forty steps in advance of me; I placed myself near
her with my two aids, one of whom had been an apothe-
cary boy at Landrecies, and the other a dentist; they
made themselves surgeons. But they already have much
experience, and with a little leisure and pains, these
young men will perhaps become something. Madame
Thérèse then kissed little Jean, who was running to join
the battalion. The whole valley, right and left, was
filled with cavalry in good order. General Hoche, on his
arrival, at once placed two batteries on the hills of
Reichshofen, and the infantry halted in the middle of
the valley. There was another consultation, then all the
infantry ranged themselves in three columns; one
passed on the left into the gorge of Réebach, the other
two marched on the intrenchments, with bayonets fixed.
General Hoche, with some officers, stationed himself on
a little elevation to the left of the valley.

"What followed, my dear friends, seems to me like a dream. At the moment when the columns reached the foot of the hill, a horrible crash, a kind of frightful tearing sound was heard; everything was covered with smoke; the Prussians had just discharged their cannon. A second afterward, as the smoke cleared away a little, we saw the French higher up the slope; they were slackening their speed, numbers of wounded were left behind, some stretched on their faces, others seated, and trying to rise.

"The Prussians fired the second time;—then was heard the terrible cry of the Republicans, ' *To the bayonet!* ' And all the mountain sparkled like firebrands when one stirs them up with his foot. We saw no more, because the wind blew the smoke toward us, nor could we hear a word at four feet distance, so loud was the firing—men and cannon thundering and roaring together.

"Our cavalry horses on the hills neighed, and tried to rush into the fight. These animals are truly savage; they love danger; it was with great difficulty that they could be restrained. Occasionally there was an opening in the smoke, and we could see the Republicans climbing the palisades like ants upon an ant-hill; some with the butt-end of their guns trying to break down the intrenchments, others seeking a passage; the colonels on horseback, their swords upraised, urged on their men, and on the other side the Prussians thrust forward their bayonets, and fired their guns into the heap of bodies, or raised their great cannon-rammers like clubs to beat down the men. It was frightful! A moment after, another gust of wind covered everything with smoke, and none could know how the struggle would end.

"General Hoche sent his officers, one after another, to take new orders; they rushed through the smoke like the wind; one would have thought them shadows. But the battle continued, and the Republicans were beginning to recoil, when the general himself came down at full gallop. Ten minutes afterward the song of the *Marseillaise* rose above all the tumult, and those who had retreated, returned to the charge. The second attack began more furiously than the first. The cannon alone still thundered, and struck down files of men. All the Republicans advanced *en masse*, Hoche in their midst. Our batteries, too, fired on the Prussians. It is impossible to describe what happened when the French were once near the palisades. If Father Adam Schmitt had been with us he would have seen what may be called a terrible battle. The Prussians showed themselves soldiers of the great Frederick; bayonets against bayonets, —sometimes one party, sometimes the other was driven back, or rushed forward.

"But what decided the victory for the Republicans, was the arrival of their third column on the heights, on the left of the intrenchments. It had turned the Réebach, and came out from the forest double quick. Then the Prussians were obliged to give up the struggle; attacked on both sides they retreated, leaving eighteen pieces of cannon, twenty-four wagons, and their intrenchments filled with the dead and wounded. They went toward Wœrth, and our hussars, beside themselves with impatience, started at last, bending forward on

their saddles. We learned that night that they had
taken twelve hundred prisoners, and six pieces of cannon.

"This, my dear friends, was the battle of Wœrth and
Froeschwiller, the news of which must have reached you
already. It will ever remain present to my mind. Since
that, I have seen nothing new. But what work we have
had! We have had to amputate, to extract balls; our
ambulances are loaded with the wounded. It is very
sad.

"Nevertheless, the day after the battle, the army
moved forward. Four days afterward we were told that
the members Lacoste and Baudot, being convinced that
the rivalry between Hoche and Pichegru was injurious
to the interests of the Republic, had given the command
entirely to Hoche, and that he, finding himself at the
head of the armies of the Rhine and Moselle, without
losing a moment, had profited by it to attack Wurmser
on the road to Wissembourg, and that we had com-
pletely routed him at Geisberg, so that now the Prussians are retreating to Mayence, the Austrians to Gemer-
sheim, and the territory of the Republic is relieved of all
its enemies.

"As for me, I am now at Wissembourg overwhelmed
with work; Madame Thérèse and little Jean, and the
remnant of the first battalion, occupy the place, and the
army is on the march to Landau, the happy deliverance
of which will be the admiration of future ages. Soon,
soon, dear friends, we will follow the army, we will pass
through Anstatt, crowned with the palms of victory.
We shall again press you to our hearts, and celebrate

with you the triumph of justice and liberty. Oh dear
liberty! rekindle in our souls the sacred fire which
formerly burned in the breasts of so many heroes. Cre-
ate among us generations which may resemble them,
that the heart of every citizen may leap at thy voice.
Inspire the wise who plan; lead the courageous to heroic
actions; animate the soldiers with a sublime enthusiasm; may despots who divide nations for the sake of op-
pressing them, disappear from the world, and may the
sacred bond of brotherhood reunite all the peoples of
the earth in one family!

" With these wishes, and these hopes, the good Madame
Thérèse, little Jean and I, embrace you with all our
hearts.   JACOB WAGNER.

" P. S.—Little Jean begs his friend Fritzel to take good
care of Scipio."

Uncle Jacob's letter filled us all with joy, and
after that you may imagine with what impatience
we awaited the arrival of the first battalion. This
epoch of my life, when I think of it, seems to me
like a fête; every day we learned something new;
after the occupation of Wissembourg came the
raising of the siege of Landau, then the capture of
Lauterbourg, then that of Kaiserslautern, and the
occupation of Spire, where the French collected
great spoils, which Hoche caused to be carried to
Landau to indemnify the inhabitants for their
losses.

The people of the village now held us in respect as much as they had formerly abused us. It was even a question with them whether they should not put Koffel in the town council, and appoint the mole-catcher burgomaster—no one knew why, for nobody had such an idea until then. But the report was spread that we were going to become Frenchmen again; we had been French fifteen hundred years before, and it was abominable that we had so long allowed ourselves to be held in slavery. Richter had taken flight, knowing very well what he might expect, and Spick no longer left his house. Every day the people on the main street looked toward the mountain to watch for the true defenders of their country. Unfortunately the greater part of the army had taken the road from Wissembourg to Mayence, leaving Anstatt on their left in the mountains. We saw stragglers pass who were taking the short road through the Burgerwald. We were much troubled, and were beginning to think that our battalion would never come, when one day the mole-catcher rushed in, breathless, crying:

" Here they are! Here they are! "

He was returning from the fields with his spade on his shoulder, and had seen a troop of soldiers

17

in the distance. The whole village had already heard the news, and came into the street. I, beside myself with enthusiasm, ran to meet the battalion, with Hans Aden and Frantz Sépel, whom I met on the road. The sun was shining, the snow was melting, the mud splashed round us like grapeshot, but we did not mind it, and ran for half an hour without stopping. Half the village, men, women, and children, followed us, shouting:

"They're coming! They're coming!"

People's ideas changed in a singular manner,— everybody was then a friend to the Republic. Once on the side of the Birkenwald, Hans, Frantz, and I at last saw our battalion marching up the declivity, their knapsacks on their backs, their guns on their shoulders, the officers behind their companies. Farther off the wagons were defiling over the great bridge. They all came on, whistling, talking, as soldiers do on the march. One stopped to light his pipe, another gave a shrug of his shoulder to raise his knapsack. We could hear gay voices and shouts of laughter, for the French when they march always tell stories and make funny speeches, to keep up their spirits.

In this crowd my eyes sought only Uncle Jacob and Madame Thérèse. It was some time before I discovered them, in the rear of the battalion. My uncle was riding Rappel. I hardly recognized him at first, for he wore a large Republican hat, a coat with red lapels, and a great sword in an iron scabbard. This costume changed him wonderfully, and made him seem much taller; but I knew him, notwithstanding, and Madame Thérèse also, in her cart covered with cloth, in the same hat and cravat in which I first saw her. She had rosy cheeks and sparkling eyes. My uncle rode near her, and they were talking together. I recognized little Jean, also, whom I had seen only once. He was marching; a large belt adorned with drum-sticks crossed his breast, his arms were covered with lace, and his sword dangled behind. And the Colonel, Sergeant Laflèche, and the captain to whom I had shown the way into our garret, and all the soldiers,—yes, nearly all,—I recognized; they seemed to me to be one great family. It gave me pleasure to see the flag covered with oil-cloth, too. I ran through the crowd. Hans Aden and Frantz Sépel had already found comrades,—but I ran on, and as I came near the cart, was going to say, " Uncle! Uncle! " when Madame Thérèse, happening to bend forward, exclaimed, joyfully:

" Here's Scipio! "

And at that moment, Scipio, whom I had forgotten and left at home, sprang into the cart, all bewildered and muddy. Little Jean immediately cried:

"Scipio!"

And the good dog, after passing his great moustache two or three times over Madame Thérèse's face, sprang to the ground and began to leap about Jean, barking, uttering cries, and acting as if he were wild with delight. All the battalion called:

"Here, Scipio! Scipio!"

My uncle had just seen me, and held out his arms to me from his horse. I seized his leg; he raised and kissed me. I saw that he was weeping, and that made me cry. He held me toward Madame Thérèse, who took me in her cart, saying:

"Good-day, Fritzel."

She seemed very happy, and kissed me with tears in her eyes.

Very soon the mole-catcher and Koffel came up and grasped my uncle's hand; then other people from the village, mixing, pell-mell, with the soldiers, who gave the men their knapsacks and guns to carry in triumph, and cried to the women—

"Hey, good mother with your pretty daughter! this way—this way!"

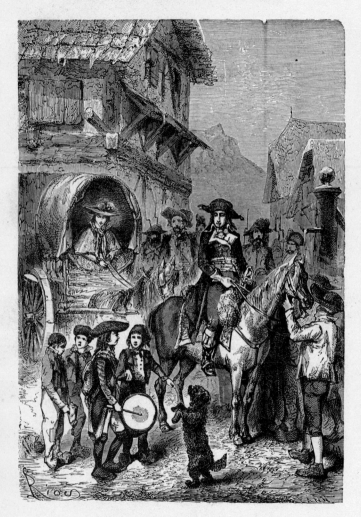

AT LAST I SAW UNCLE; HE WAS MOUNTED ON RAPPEL.

There was great confusion; everybody fraternized, and in the midst of all, little Jean and I knew not which was the happiest.

" Kiss little Jean," cried Uncle Jacob.

" Kiss Fritzel," said Madame Thérèse.

And we embraced, looking at each other in bewildered delight.

" *Il me plait*," cried little Jean, " *il a l'air bon enfant*."

" *Toi, tu me plais aussi*," said I, very proud of speaking French.

And we walked along arm-in-arm, while Uncle Jacob and Madame Thérèse looked at each other and smiled.

The Colonel, also, gave me his hand, saying:

" Ha! Dr. Wagner, here's your defender. You're quite well, my brave fellow?"

" Yes, Colonel."

" So much the better!"

In this manner we reached the first houses of the village. Then we stopped a few minutes to get in order. Little Jean hung his drum over his shoulder, and as the commander cried " Forward! March!" the drums sounded.

We marched down the main street in regular order, delighted at making so imposing an entrance.

All the old men and women who could not get out, were at their windows, and pointed to Uncle Jacob, who advanced with a dignified air behind the Colonel, between his two assistants. I noticed Father Schmitt particularly, standing at his door; he straightened up his tall, bent figure, and watched us filing past, with sparkling eyes.

At the square with the fountain the Colonel cried:

" Halt! "

They stacked their guns, and all dispersed, right and left. Each citizen wished to have a soldier; all wanted to rejoice in the triumph of the Republic, " one and indivisible." But these Frenchmen, with their cheerful faces, preferred to follow the pretty girls. The Colonel went with us. Old Lisbeth was already at the door, her hands raised to heaven, and cried:

" Ah Madame Thérèse!—ah *monsieur le docteur!* "

There were fresh cries of joy, fresh embraces.

Then we went in, and the feast of ham, chitterlings, and broiled meat, with white wine and old Burgundy to drink, began; Koffel, the mole-catcher, the Colonel, little Jean and I,—I leave you to imagine the table. the appetites, the satisfaction!

All that day the first battalion remained with us; then they were obliged to pursue their march, for their winter quarters were at Hacmatt, two short leagues from Anstatt. My uncle stayed in the village. He laid aside his great sword and large hat; but from that time until spring not a day passed that he did not go to Hacmatt; he thought of nothing but Hacmatt.

Madame Thérèse came to see us occasionally with little Jean. We laughed, we were happy and we loved each other!

What more shall I say? In the spring, when the lark began to sing, we heard one day that the first battalion was going to leave for La Vendée. Then my uncle, very pale, ran to the stable, and mounted Rappel; he rode off at full speed, bareheaded, having forgotten to put on his cap.

What passed at Hacmatt? I know nothing about it. But what I am sure of is that the next day my uncle returned, as proud as a king, with Madame Thérèse and little Jean; that there was a great feast at our house, kisses and rejoicing.

Eight days afterward Colonel Duchêne arrived with all the captains of the battalion. That day there were still greater rejoicings. Madame Thérèse and Uncle Jacob went to the mayoralty, followed by a long procession of joyous guests. The mole-catcher, who had been chosen burgomaster by popular vote, awaited us in his tri-colored scarf. He entered my uncle's and Madame Thérèse's names in a thick register, to everybody's satisfaction. And from that time little Jean had a father, and I had a good mother, whose memory I cannot recall without shedding tears.

There are many more things I should like to tell you—but this is enough for one time. If the good God permits, we will one day continue this story, which ends,—like all others,—with white hairs, and the last adieus of those whom we love best in the world.